Twitterature

The World's Greatest Books
in Twenty Tweets or Less

ALEXANDER ACIMAN

AND

EMMETT RENSIN

PENGUIN BOOKS

PENGUIN BOOKS

Published by the Penguin Group
Penguin Group (USA) Inc., 375 Hudson Street, New York, New York 10014, U.S.A.
Penguin Group (Canada), 90 Eglinton Avenue East, Suite 700, Toronto,
Ontario, Canada M4P 2Y3 (a division of Pearson Penguin Canada Inc.)
Penguin Books Ltd, 80 Strand, London WC2R 0RL, England
Penguin Ireland, 25 St Stephen's Green, Dublin 2, Ireland
(a division of Penguin Books Ltd)
Penguin Group (Australia), 250 Camberwell Road, Camberwell,
Victoria 3124, Australia (a division of Pearson Australia Group Pty Ltd)
Penguin Books India Pvt Ltd, 11 Community Centre,
Panchsheel Park, New Delhi – 110 017, India
Penguin Group (NZ), 67 Apollo Drive, Rosedale, North Shore 0632,
New Zealand (a division of Pearson New Zealand Ltd)
Penguin Books (South Africa) (Pty) Ltd, 24 Sturdee Avenue,
Rosebank, Johannesburg 2196, South Africa

Penguin Books Ltd, Registered Offices: 80 Strand, London WC2R 0RL, England

First published in Penguin Books 2009

1 3 5 7 9 10 8 6 4 2

Copyright © Alexander Aciman and Emmett L. Rensin, 2009
All rights reserved

LIBRARY OF CONGRESS CATALOGING IN PUBLICATION DATA
Aciman, Alexander.
Twitterature : the world's greatest books in twenty tweets or less /
Alexander Aciman and Emmett Rensin.
p.   cm.
ISBN 978-0-14-311732-2
1. Best books—Humor.   2. Twitter.   I. Rensin, Emmett.   II. Title.
PN6231.B62A36 2009
818'.607—dc22   2009040344

Printed in the United States of America

PENGUIN BOOKS

TWITTERATURE

"The classics are so last century." —*The Guardian*

"Sincerest apologies to Shakespeare, Stendhal, and Joyce: how were we to know it would come to this?" —Mashable.com

"The trouble with Twitter is, I think, that too many twits might make a twat." —David Cameron

"*Twitterature* makes me want to punch someone, preferably the 'authors.' They're in Chicago. I'm gonna take a road trip." —@damig, Twitter

"A move likely to be greeted by book lovers with a mixture of horror and why-didn't-I-think-of-that jealousy." —*Chicago Tribune*

"Just f*#%ing shoot me now." —Mike C., grouchyconservativepundits.com

ALEXANDER ACIMAN was born in 1990. A sophomore at the University of Chicago, he was graduated from Horace Mann School in New York City. He has worked in the offices of several publications, including *The Paris Review* and the late *New York Sun,* which he and the city of New York mourn every day upon noticing its absence from every newsstand as the copper sun rises to greet the metropolis. He has published many articles in both his high school and college newspapers, as well as three feature article-essays in *The New York Times* and one in *The New York Sun.* He is also a devoted follower of Napoleon Bonaparte. He believes that there is no better way to start a day than with a run or a bike ride, and is known on occasion to enjoy a game of bocce or to engage in pugilism. He would like to write, own a pair of John Lobb shoes, and live out his days reading and writing in the Mediterranean basin with his brothers.

EMMETT RENSIN was born in 1990. He is a sophomore at the University of Chicago, before which he attended the finest parochial school in all of Los Angeles. A Huffington Post contributor and ordained reverend, and unable to tie his shoelaces at the tender age of sixteen, he gave it all up to pursue his true dream: putting stickers on books. This he did with care and devotion for many long hours, ensuring that every book in the reference library of the world-renowned Museum of Jurassic Technology at which he was employed had its lovely laminated ascension number neatly stuck upon its spine. He emerged from this a brighter and more worldly man. Rensin contributes to the University of Chicago's *Chicago Maroon* as well as the Huffington Post but takes care to balance his stresses with the relaxing arts of coat collection and Richard Nixon enthusiasm. Such balance is necessary, as extremity might cause Rensin's untimely death and prevent him from accomplishing his three life goals: penning the Great American Novel, mastery of card magic, and telling the perfect shaggy-dog joke.

*Dedicated in Loving Memory
to the Victims of the R.M.S.* Titanic

Contents

Introduction

Life can offer us no greater treasure than art. It is all that is beautiful, and all that allows a man's soul to take leave of the quotidian trifles that molest his waking mind, to be lifted to the highest peaks of experience, and to peer briefly into the sublime. It is that which removes man from the static residue of time and casts him into the gentle waters of the eternal. It is to hear and to speak softly in the beauteous tongue of antiquity, and yet to foresee all that will unfold through the illimitably growing passage of our universe.

In short, art is pretty sweet.

What a *tragédie*, then, that so many modern people find the great works of literature inaccessible, overwhelming, and even, perhaps, dull. It is not a defect of their character, nor any special ineptitude that has disposed them in this manner; rather, these great texts – timeless as they may be – are, in their present form, outdated. Who but college students, hermits, and disciples of the disgraced John Ludd can muddle through them with any hope of understanding? This is what we seek, through our humble efforts, to remedy.

While some may describe the reinvention of our world's Great Works to suit the ever-evolving brain of the modern man as 'a triviality', 'a travesty', or 'that sucks', we prefer to think of ourselves as modern-day Martin Luthers. Herr Luther took the Holy Scripture itself, and seeing that the classic Vulgate no longer spoke to the souls of his contemporaries, he translated it into the vernacular of his time. By doing so, Luther unleashed a revolution of faith and literacy upon sixteenth-century Europe that had not been seen before and has not been equaled since.

In our own way, and in our own time, we hope to do the same.

However, it's probably best if we stay clear of the Bible.

You may be wondering, good sirs, what exactly we intend to do with these great works of art. What one must keep in mind is that the literary canon is not valued for its tens of thousands of dull, dull words but for the raw insight into humanity it provides. While perhaps an unwieldy tome was the best method of digesting this knowledge during a summer spent in the Victorian countryside in the Year of Our Lord, Eighteen Hundred and Seventy-Three, times have changed. Virginity must not be distracted with books, nor damsel-chasing pacified with poetry. Instead we must run free into the world and not once look back.

And so, we give you the means to absorb the

strong voices, valuable lessons and stylistic innovations of the Greats without the burdensome duty of hours spent reading. We take these Great Works and present their most essential elements, distilled into the voice of Twitter – *the social networking tool that with its limit of 140 characters a post (including spaces) has refined to its purest form the instant-publishing, short-attention-span, all-digital-all-the-time, self-important age of info-deluge* – and give you everything you need to master the literature of the civilized world.

For indeed, does any man have such great pretense as to suppose that he may digest all that it is right and proper for him to have digested in the stunted mortal fit granted to him by Providence? Perhaps in the eighteenth year of your life you sat on a porch asking yourself: *What exactly is Hamlet trying to tell me? Why must he mince words and muse in lyricism and, in short, whack about the shrub?* Such questions are no doubt troubling – and we believe they would have been resolved were the Prince of Denmark a registered user on Twitter.com, well versed in the idiosyncrasies and idioms of the modern day. And this, in essence, is what we have done. We have liberated poor Hamlet from the rigorous literary constraints of the sixteenth century and made him – without losing an ounce of wisdom, beauty, wit, or angst – a happening youngster. Just like you, dear reader.

In brief – and we mean this literally – we have created our generation's salvation, a new and revolutionary way of facing and understanding the greatest art of all arts: Literature.

And allow us now to open
The eternal aperture,
To the brilliant soul of common man:
We now present you . . . *Twitterature*.

The Catcher in the Rye
by J. D. Salinger

@HoldenLolfield

Fucked up for the last time. They're throwin' me out of the old school! Still haven't seen a goddamn horse! LOL!

Do you ever wonder what they used in Egypt to embalm mummies? It's special ancient mummy juice, that's what it is.

Left school. Totally yelled some nasty shit down the hall – that'll show em! Headin' 2 NY soon. Hit me up.

Surrounded by phonies. Everywhere!

I tried to bone some kid's mom. She wasn't havin' it. I have this really gay lumberjack hat now, though.

Checked into a dingy hotel; it's pretty crappy. Pay per view isn't working. I guess I'll just call a hooker?

Whoa: never ever try to short a hooker. These guys called pimps come and fuck you up.

Still surrounded by phonies! I bet you're all phonies, too. Ugh.

Think I have mouth cancer – will keep you all updated.

Anyone know where ducks go during winter? Do they freeze??

On a date with a girl I don't care about. So bizarre that nature makes me do such funny, contradictory things. Hypocrisy to the max. Deep.

- -

Decided to run away from home. I told my sister about it. She's here.

- -

I think some dude just tried to fuck me. Yeah, some dude just tried to put his dick in me. Disgusting.

- -

He's a phony too, of course.

- -

Sister insists on going west with me – I said no way. Women can't be cowboys!!

- -

On second thought, west probably as phony as east.

- -

Life is full of frustration and contradiction.

- -

I miss those pricks I swore at in school. :(Even though they were phonies.

- -

The Da Vinci Code
by Dan Brown

@CatholicGuilt

Heading to Paris! A man is dead and the police think only my superhuman knowledge of cryptology can solve this one.

Oh fuck – the police think I killed him!!!

These idiots don't understand this is a CODE! Thankfully, this bangin' – er, beautiful – French girl is helping me out.

Driving to a bank. Good time to exposit the history of all these crazy Catholic secret societies to this French girl – maybe get her hot??

HOLY SHIT!!!! We stole the Codex for a large-scale conspiracy that is conveniently in my area of expertise!

A historian explained rest of complicated conspiratorial legend. It's good we keep track of all this. For the lady's benefit, of course.

WTF!! A FUCKING ALBINO!! My cushy tenure at Harvard did NOT prepare me for all this action!!!

You know that old Italian dude who painted the picture of the smiling lady? He's the key to all of this. LOL, who would have thought?

Police won't stop chasing us! Will tweet all locations; just don't tell the Popo! Or the Pope.

Oh man, this gal is hot. But it's harder than I thought to find romance amidst a global plot to conceal the truth about Jesus Christ.

Taking a breather to solve some puzzles. 'A Pope', anybody? There's so many! Mad props if anyone can solve it.

Thanks to @dudeonthebus. Oh goddamnit, another cryptex? Jesus fucking Christ. Literally.

Can't someone tell this albino and the cops that we're just TRYING TO SOLVE A MYSTERY? It's like a crossword! Everyone needs to CTFO!

Puzzles, puzzles, puzzles all day long.

So you're looking for something. Got a smokin' hot French babe with you. Then it turns out what you're looking for IS that babe. Yeah!

Jesus. The lady is a direct descendant of Christ. All good. Oh what? Another puzzle? Bring on the sequel!

Paradise Lost
by John Milton

@MorningStarlet

FALLING UNTO THE ABYSS!!!!! I'll talk more about why in
several hundred pages to avoid any confusion.

OH MY GOD I'M IN HELL.

'Tis Pandemonium down here. Would ROFL but it's
very hot.

I'm bored. I'm the chairman of the board. My compatriots
are r-tards. Inaction? Is that the best we can do? We art
fucking demons!

Sitting on our asses waiting for an apology from G–d isn't
exactly renegade. Pussies.

Anyone heard anything about Earth? Good? Bad? Will be
there tonight bringing the MOTHAFUCKIN' RUCKUS. If
anyone wants in, txt it.

On second thought, I'm going alone.

So there was a fight. Sometimes you invent gunpowder
and you think SWEET but then they whip out JESUS CHRIST
HIMSELF and BAM! We're in hell.

How do you defeat your own son, born to YOUR OWN
DAUGHTER! Freud would have a field day.

Did you know I can change shapes? BAM: halo, wings, grace. Looking sharp, looking the part. Time to go kick some Promethean ass.

What? The almighty knows everything? Asshole sent Gabriel – the mothafuckin' archangel himself – to warn Adam and his first lady.

It's comforting to know that women were just man's first really good idea.

I'd like to cite Angry Mob v. Frankenstein – we are not responsible for all your nonsense.

Turns out the woman's dumber than the man, but she has this thing that if she doesn't give it to him, he starts to obey. I shall exploit that.

Dressed as a snake. She's going for it . . . Yes! She ate the forbidden apple! Guess God wasn't paying attention. Omniscient, hah!

So I won. They're getting kicked out. Boo hoo.

They're holding hands and crying. I wish someone would hold my hand :(

Beelzebub just isn't what I want. Stop crying! I didn't cry when I got kicked out of heaven and lost Parad— I FOUND A NAME FOR MY MEMOIRS!!

The Metamorphosis
by Franz Kafka

@bugged-out

Another day. Gotta go out selling.

Typing feels weird today.

Uh-oh. There are some white spots on my stomach . . .

I seem to have transformed into a large bug. Has this ever happened to any of you? No solution on Web MD.

This Is so weird. I read that this kind of thing usually reflects a deep disgust and discomfort with one's body. Is this true? Ana/Mia/bug??

Family not happy with my condition! Father and mother may want me dead.

Sister leaves me food!!! Thank god.

Sorry no updates. Bug time is weird. Lose track.

Sister very timid and confused – what's up with that? – but still leaving me food.

Looked outside today. Men living in my house! Who let them in? Sis plays violin for them! MORE DEGRADING THAN BEING AN INSECT.

That's it. I'm going out there. Wish me luck.

OMFG, my father totally threw an apple into my back.

REPEAT: THERE IS AN APPLE LODGED IN MY FUCKIN' BACK!

I am dying – the pain grows greater every day.

If I die my family may be able to move on. I curse the day I inexplicably transformed into a gigantic, six-legged metaphor!

And the rest is silence . . .

(Now that I'm gone my sister is a capable woman with a promising future. Guess the real 'metamorphosis' was hers!)

The Stranger
by Albert Camus

@TheRiskofSyphilis

Mom dead. Not sure if it was today or yesterday.

At the funeral now. Bored. People seem sad. Text, don't call. This old man was totally schtupping mom!

Funeral took forever. Spotted a woman on the way home. Will see her tomorrow, maybe get lucky.

At the beach, day is hot. I guess I find myself aroused by Marie – I guess.

Jesus, Raymond hit his woman again. Apparently we're friends.

Making omelets. Marie drops L-bomb. Too soon I think! Why must women always play hate 'n' shit?

Work sucks. Boss is such a douche. Don't worry, I'm not moving!!

Marie's gotten over herself. Women. Going to the beach with Raymond and her.

God, it's hot. Long ride. Lunch soon.

DRRRRUNNNKKKKK!!!!!!!!!

Atmosphere heavy, taking a walk. Taking the revolver too, Arabs abroad. Still hot and still drunk. Good combination.

9

The sun is oppressive and sickening. Becoming mad. Fever from the light, and eyes are tired.

Arab in the distance. Those folks are trouble. KNIFE! THIS SHIT JUST GOT HEAVY!!!

May have shot Arab. Four times. The heat had beaten madness into my brow. Who's got 200 francs for bail?

Trial starting today. Why does everyone tell me I didn't do it? They ask if I am sure.

Just finished my statement. Told it all like it was. Lawyer seems regretful, judge angry, Marie wistful. I am confused.

Priest still bothering me. I feel guilty without knowing it (nor will I ever) then yelled at him until I was called a devil. What a tool.

It is such a burden to see Marie, although it comforts me. She may stop coming one day.

Big day tomorrow. Feeling pretty good. One last favor: please come to the execution. Represent with your howls of hatred.

Found an exit.

Oedipus the King
by Sophocles

@WhathappensinThebes . . .

Ever have weird flashes of memory from childhood, like getting tied to a tree in a forest and crawling a hundred miles to safety?

I have a lot of weird thoughts herding sheep all day. Boring, boring, boring. Shit, someone's coming . . .

It's the king! He's yelling at me as the sheep bleat and I tweet. Cell phone use probably upsetting both.

If someone tries to kill you but you kill them first, that's self-defense right? Even if you're a shepherd and they're, uh, King of Thebes?

Anybody have Johnnie Cochran's number?

PARTY IN THEBES!!!!! Nobody cares I killed that old dude, plus this woman is ALL OVER ME! Total MILF.

Who's the DJ In this place? Why does he keep playing 'The End' by The Doors?

Who are these people who keep coming up behind me singing ominous choral pieces? I'm busy trying to mack here!

Hey, this lady is the queen. Getting some royal booty. Weird: She seems not the least bit upset that I killed her old husband!

- -

Slow day preparing to be king.

- -

ACK! Having more flashes of childhood memory. I see my parents arguing about some prophecy where I kill them. Is it just me, or . . . ?

- -

These bizarre emotions have opened a whole new bag of issues. Must tell Sigmund next session to forget about abandonment and focus on this.

- -

Oh my God. These people will NOT stop singing behind me. SHUT UP! SHUT UP! BTW: How do they know my name?

- -

An old guy outside the palace keeps yelling about 'your mother' . . . 'killed your father' . . . 'inces—' well, shit.

- -

MY EYES MY FUCKING EYES AGGGGHGHGHGHGHGHHHH!!!!!! I was totally not expecting that to hurt so much.

- -

Oh well. Must keep on trucking to Colonus. Wish I had a seeing-eye dog. Glad I learned touch-typing.

- -

Childe Harold's Pilgrimage
by Lord Byron

@GreekWithEnvy

While my senses bend at the sublime,
And quake before the ocean's trepidation . . .

My spirit blazes wrath of the divine,
Soars greatly, loves, swoons, rages, and bangs your wife.

Lost 100 followers with those last two!! Sorry guys!!! Will try to be more direct!

My journey has begun. I've set off into the world with 100 gallons of ink and paper. My companion is vomiting overboard.

I grow weary of Englishmen. They have no appreciation for the vastness of the earth. Wine, servant, MORE WINE! Going on a bender tonight.

What a world we've been given! Were I God himself I could not engineer one finer than this!

The wind caresses my face like the arse-fart of a Peloponnesian princess.

Today I ate six biscuits, boxed an hour, and wrote a letter to Napoleon.

Met an Albanian leader. What wisdom inhabits him! Yet he does enjoy killing the innocent for no reason at all. We have become close friends.

Tambourgi! Tambourgi! the Albanian minstrels chant. I do believe that knowing this song gives me immediate insight into their world.

Greece. Note to self: upon arrival home, seduce sister.

These Greek eight-year-olds in my garden are H–A–U–G–H–T HOT.

Second note to self: try to separate real life and poem to avoid confusion. Maybe change name from Byron to Harold?

I've purchased traditional clothing. These local women fall at my knees and beg to be my concubines.

I have grown to love this part of the world, and how much richer and more tender it is than England.

Also, got a sweet tan from the Aegean sun. FTW.

Keep posted for the next two cantos in six years.

I hope I don't get distracted by a wife in that time. Gosh, I would be the worst husband ever. But I'm a great lover. Isn't that ironic?

You know what would really put a halt to my poetic aspirations? Tuberculosis. Oh Keats, thank god I won't end up that way.

It's all this Mediterranean air that's keeping me safe. Yes, I definitely can't get tuberculosis down here.

Slaughterhouse Five
by Kurt Vonnegut

@allesuberdeutschland

Welcome to my great war Twitter!

. . . unsure what to post next. Old buddy no help. Any suggestions?

I think I'm unstuck from time. Will this screw up my feed?

This is a crazy journey! Isn't my name – Pilgrim – just so fitting for this? Just so you know, Dresden is totally getting bombed.

So it goes.

The army is tough. I'm so not cut out for this! Somebody get me out of here.

War doesn't suck. It goes.

Oh man, I just met these aliens from Tralfamadore, and they see time totally different.

Aliens are a perfect insightful foil for the horrific violence brought on by the human condition. AND THEY'VE GOT EYE-STALKS!!

Stuck behind the lines. When are the aliens coming back? I'm cold and everyone here is a simple portrait of life. Becoming very cynical.

Captured by Nazis. So it goes.

With the aliens again. Or I am very old. Or very young. A less clever literary device would be much less upsetting to my stomach!

Dresden is such a beautiful city! I'll have to show my grandkids!

I'm stuck in a meat locker. The city is being bombed. Not sure if this will upload. Wish me luck!

Tralfamadorians look like toilet plungers. They want to watch me get it on with hot chick. Flush that! Night curtain please.

Everything destroyed. War is terrible. Can you all not see how terrible war is? My survival is an accident.

The world is cruel. The bombs have left a permanent mark on my psyche!

I am just a baby.

So it goes.

Harry Potter (1–7)
by J. K. Rowling

@NotoriousHP

Hello everyone from under the stairs! Aunt and Uncle threw me under here again. Gosh, life is so hard.

That fat fuck Dudley stole all my food! I wish something good or at least interesting would happen to me.

OMG I'm a WIZARD! And my parents are DEAD WIZARDS! Off to magic boarding school. PEACE BITCHES!

OMG Hogwarts OMG I have two friends OMG magic OMG the Slytherins are Nazis OMG there is an EVIL WIZARD out to get me.

Snape a douche! Dumbledore a wise man (but maybe gay?). Voldemort tried to kill me! Flying broomstick! Battle over magic crack-rock!

OMG the year's over. Time goes fast when you're having fun. Goes slow if you have to read seven books with lots of adverbs.

Back to school! Should be a great year! I hope nothing crazy happens like last time.

No! Voledemort is trying to wreck my shit up AGAIN!! I am TIRED of these MOTHERFUCKING SNAKES IN THIS MOTHERFUCKING CASTLE!

Back to school AGAIN! This year definitely better! A dude who tried to kill me turned out OK. Sometimes misunderstandings happen. LOL.

- -

Oh man, big tournament at my school!! PSYCHED! I hope nobody dies this year, and every year as if by clockwork.

- -

Competing in a tournament. Also: is it just me, or should they really have a tougher vetting process for Dark Arts teachers?

- -

OMFG VOLDEMORT AGAIN. Don't worry, I have the hang of this by now. Plus there's a secret society out to protect me. Give up already LV.

- -

I AM UNDERGOING A LOT OF ANGST RIGHT NOW. And this Asian girl is giving me a major hard-on. Blue balls suck. No magic potion for it either.

- -

Don't believe anyone who says Voldemort isn't back AGAIN. I KNOW WHAT I SAW!

- -

Big brawl at Ministry of Magic! Sirius is dead. Super-pissed. I just used the torture spell, didn't I? I'm going to Azkaban now, aren't I?

- -

Back to school again! Boy, everything better go well this year or I'm going to eat a wand.

- -

Hey! My friend's sister is totally hot for me. Feels a bit dirty, but yeah baby, you like my scar, don't you? Wanna see my wand?

- -

SNAPE KILLED DUMBLEDORE WTF WTF WTF WTF WTF? THIS IS LIKE THE BIGGEST CLIFFHANGER EVER!!!

Sometimes this guy, Tom, keeps showing up. I don't want him around but I don't have the heart to tell him, because he killed my parents.

NM last tweet. Killed him. Something about a prophecy. Who cares? Last seven years have felt like same one, over and over.

The Red and the Black
by Stendhal

@Byrony

My new black robes can pass as the most austere in all the region. The maid went to town today.

Moved into the Mayor's house to tutor kids. Wife mistook me for a starving peasant girl.

Impressed everyone by memorizing Bible. Winged it on Horace, though. Easy to know Latin when nobody else knows it.

Wife insulted my dignity, suggested I buy new linens. Told her off though!

Mayor displeased by my treatment of his wife. What a downer. Yelled at him too. Got a raise, big time.

Wife over it. Totally wants my babies. Though beautiful, can't say I'm feeling it.

On second thought, it's my duty to seduce her, isn't it? Hypocrisy drives me. It's a point of honor.

Grabbed her hand in the garden, freaked out, and forced her. Got it on.

Been too busy to post. Torrid affair. Kinky. Much like Napoleon's conquest of Spain, really.

I've been discovered, must move to Paris to work with a Marquis. Hope he has a hot wife . . . or daughter.

Daughter. Schwing! Score!

Went six to noon today thinking about Napoleon. What a guy.

I'm on this ladder, right? Just trying to get some action and next thing I know I'm bleeding on the floor. FML.

I believe I've finally earned the Marquis' trust.

Oops. His daughter is pregz. I swear I'm not the daddy!!!

Mayor's wife totally blew my cover. I've gotten pistols made. Must take her out.

Backfired. She's not dead, and I'm on trial.

She's trying to free me, but no, I've got a duty to truth and society. I tell the court what happened. Might not be able to post for a while.

In jail. It blows. Guard's an ass. Time to repent soon, but I'm not going for it. I wonder if this will inspire a book. Or a movie. With Leo.

Today is the sentencing. I am guilty. Women fill the courtroom, bawling. My, it's two o'clock in the afternoon.

Macbeth
by William Shakespeare

@BigMAC

Battle went well! Cut mothafuckas from the nave to the chops! Neither bade farewell nor shook hands. WORD UP! REPRESENT!

Away to home now with my homeboy Banquo. I shall be in Inverness in time for haggis.

ZOUNDS! OLD HAGS SAY I SHALL BE KING AND SHITE. THEN I TOTALLY BECAME THANE OF CAWDOR!

Playing it cool, but I am suddenly filled with a deep ambition. 'Tis bad news.

Home now. Lady Macbeth hot over coming power/my nads. She wants to kill Duncan TONIGHT. Can't tell if she's serious or just into dirty-talk.

She was serious. Women, LOL.

Things do move so fast! The official tweets of we, the King of Scotland. Yet I fear Banquo knows my terrible secret.

Royal banquet tonight! All commanded to come! I *especially* look forward to seeing my dear friend Banquo! Hope you make it cos'!!

Banquo seems to have died in the forest. Oh well!

Everyone is leaving the party!! What? WHAT? Does no one else see BLEEDING GODDAMN BANQUO AT THE TABLE?

I'm trying to sleep. Will someone please shut this wino up? I'm the king goddamn it, can't I get a reliable porter? Seriously.

Old Hags say Macbeth is killed by no man of woman born. Relieved. The Terminator not invented yet.

My enemies and their families keep dying randomly! This is beginning to get out of hand. Nah, my wife is definitely right about this.

Maybe not. Wife is having midlife crisis or woman troubles. Bitch is nuts.

@LadyMac: THERE'S NOTHING ON YOUR HANDS, YOU'VE WASHED THEM 100 TIMES ALREADY!!

People found out about the whole murder thing; they're all pissed. I say everyone must chill out and stop blowing shit out of proportion.

Armies moving against me, Queen's dead. Life is nothing but a lone poster, tweeting his time upon the stage and then he tweets no more!

Hah! Macduff thinks he can kill me!

Shit. 'C-Section' is not 'of woman born'? What kind of king dies on a goddamn technicality?

The Hobbit
by J. R. R. Tolkien

@BilboBangin'

The Shire is so BORING. Boring boring boring. Plus all the chicks are so short!

This old dude wants me to throw a party for some dwarves. Couldn't hurt. Plus, I'm gonna get WASTED.

Last time I drank so much I woke up still in the tavern . . . keeper's wife! ZING!

Crap. I seem to have been fandangled into a daring adventure to some mountain. Do I have to?

Walking walking walking . . .

Still walking – this is so boring!

Stopped and ate at Elf City. Must everyone ALWAYS ask me if I have a normal-sized penis? Do elves have normal sized ears? No. STFU.

Walking . . .

Oh shit! This Hobbit is on crack and he has a magic ring that makes you INVISIBLE!

Got the ring. Man that guy was crazy! Probably not connected to this sweet magic ring, right?

Walking some more. Do these dwarves never get tired of walking? At least I've got this, pretty, precious, sweet . . . wonderful, amazing ring.

Waaaallllkkkiiiiinnn! Oh, wait. Stopped to eat.

Eating a sandwich – really good.

Taking a shit – really good.

Goddamn it. We're walking again. Deep forests. Endless mountains. Bad reception.

First, let me tell you about the sky . . . and then the tree line . . . and then the rocks . . . and then the ground . . . zzzz.

Walking still.

Eating again.

OH SHIT A HUGE BATTLE! IF ONLY THIS HAD HAPPENED EARLIER I WOULDN'T HAVE BEEN SO FUCKING BORED!

A Portrait of the Artist as a Young Man
by James Joyce

@Bildungsroman

I'm a young child now. Isn't that obvious from all my nursery rhymes? Tralalalalala.

Parents arguing at the table. Dad's one stubborn bastard. But I got a cool uncle. Nobody rebels against cool uncles.

I'm a bit older now. All I do is read books. School blows, kids are such assholes. They mock me for loving Byron.

You know what makes a girl hot? White, white hands. God how I love hands. Even the schoolmaster's hands comfort me.

I just want to be a poet! WON'T THEY LEAVE ME ALONE!??!

The director is giving me special attention. I'm a special kid. Special as in unique and sharp, not retarded.

At a Jesuit retreat. Total yawn. If I hear about Hell's infinitely widening mouth or eternal grains of sand again I'm gonna eat a gun.

So hard. Trying to combat religious influences. Struggling profoundly. Seems this duality will torment me. Forever.

I'm in college. Cool. But I live at home with mom. That doesn't make me a tool, does it?

Nah, I'm totally cool. Look, I've got this cool tweed hat. Yeah, I'm cool. Totally.

All grown men still get bathed by their mothers, right? Come on. What am I supposed to do about those hard-to-reach places?

INSPIRATION! Time to write a poem. Have to go to school. Physics requirement completely killing me.

I'm on a walk with my friends. Goddamn, this walk is so long, its like, two chapters long.

I see a woman I have known for a while. I'm in love.

Poetry fills each corner of crafted consequence buried deeply in memory and deeply buried in gentle life with each thought lent to eternity.

I'm glad this whole narrative thing is coming so naturally, and didn't take a decade of work and drink and poverty.

Writing is pretty awesome, isn't it? Plus chicks dig writers. And I'm a writer. Yeah.

The Great Gatsby
by F. Scott Fitzgerald

@West-Egg

Got the new place today – kind of small, but great view! Not that I'm judging anything . . .

Visiting Daisy and her douchebag husband. They're happy but her superficiality and his stubbornness are all that is wrong with rich America.

Tom is totally having an affair and EVERYBODY knows it. Open your eyes bitch . . .

Some dude is standing on the bay with his arms up looking at a symbolic light. The Midwest didn't have so many metaphors! What a CREEP!

NEVER MIND! THIS GUY KNOWS HOW TO PAAARRRR-TTTTYYYY!! Quick: Gatsby's house!!! Txt for directions!

Sorry I haven't updated more; between my lady friend and the G-Money, I hardly have time! Did you know he got a medal from little Montenegro?

BFF Gatsby and I going to town today – should be fun! Wants me to meet his friends . . .

The World Series is fixed. Every year. Don't money and power come honestly in this country???

Gatsby wants to meet Daisy. Weird. Oh well – no reason more friends can't kick it.

Oh shit. This is a lot heavier than I expected. Why do these people keep sleeping with everyone? Keep it simple – that's what I say!

Going downtown for the day – it is so hot out!!

Everyone is yelling and fighting, it's very confusing. And it is hot! I feel like I have nothing to do with any of this!!!

Two bad drivers met. :O

Gatsby is so emo. Who cries about his girlfriend while eating breakfast . . . IN THE POOL?

For that matter, who gets shot in the pool? Gatsby and the American Dream are dead.

I'll be back in the Midwest next week – New York is nothing but one giant display of the sad and cyclical nature of the past!!

The Iliad
by Homer

@RageAgainstTheAchaean

Pissed. I am so, so very pissed.

First I have to go to this beach. Then I have to kill all these dudes. And NOW – now! This prick stole my biscuit. Who does that?

Can't resolve this problem on my own – calling Mom!

Watchin' all my dudes dyin' without my help. LOL.

Mom unable to resolve problem for me with the big fish.

WHY DOES NOBODY UNDERSTAND ME????? Only Patroclus, my . . . cousin, understands me!

Sittin' on the beach playing sad songs. Oh, my tortured soul. 'Just sittin' on the beach of the Aegean, wastin' tiiimmmmeeee . . .'

Hey, just noticed there's a million crows flying over me.

I AM SO ANGRY.

Odysseus and Phoenix came to talk sense into me. Had a tantrum. Phoenix, isn't that a cool name? I wouldn't fuck with a guy named Phoenix.

Still won't fight. I'll show them! The Gods won't even LET THEM win until I fight! One day we're going to look back on this and laugh.

Wait, where'd my armor go?

PATROCLUS!!!!! This is BULLSHIT, my . . . cousin is dead and I am SO ANGRY. I JUST FEEL LIKE DESECRATING A TEMPLE.

Brb, need to go wrestle a river god.

Watch Hector run. Going around the walls of Troy, what a tool. Doesn't anybody believe in prophecies nowadays??

PWNT. Draggin' Hector's corpse around the city. TOTALLY AWESOME!

Took the body back to camp – not decaying. His old man wants it back – can't decide whether to give it up. Can I phone a friend???

Hamlet
by William Shakespeare

@OedipusGothplex

My royal father gone and nobody seems to care.

Mom says to stop wearing black.

STOP TRYING TO CONTROL ME. I won't conform! I wish my skin would just . . . melt.

I'm too sad to notice that Ophelia's so sexy and fine. And mother also looks rather fair despite all her struggles.

AN APPARITION! This shit just got HEAVY. Apparently people don't accidentally fall on bottles of poison.

Why is Claudius telling me what to do again? YOU'RE NOT MY REAL DAD! In fact you killed my real dad. :(

2bornt2b? Can one tweet beyond the mortal coil?

I wrote a play. I hope everyone comes tonight! 7pm! Tickets are free w/ great sense of irony.

Uncle just confessed to Dad's murder.

I had a knife to that fat asshole but bitched out. Now he's alive and still taking to bed with that beautiful wo— . . . er, my mother.

Gonna try to talk some sense into Mom because boyfriend totally killed Dad. I sense this is the moment of truth, the moment of candor and –

WTF IS POLONIUS DOING BEHIND THE CURTAIN???

I just killed my girlfriend's dad. Does this mean I can't hit that?

Rosencrantz and Guildenstern are here, up to their shenanigans. YAWN.

Rosencrantz and Guildenstern are dead. Anyone miss them? Didn't think so.

The gravedigger's comic speech isn't funny at all. It's heavy and meaningful. I am so borrredddd.

Ophelia just pulled a Virginia Woolf. Funeral is on the way.

Laertes Is unhappy that I killed his father and sister. What a drama queen! Oh well, fight this evening.

Anybody want a drink? Uh–oh. That went poorly.

@PeopleofDenmark Don't worry. Fortinbras will take care of thee. Peace.

The Overcoat
by Nikolai Gogol

@StaticBureaucracy

Does anyone ever notice how it doesn't matter where you work; what matters is that it's crap?

I don't get paid enough. Nobody pays attention to me. And today was my birthday. Anybody even following my tweets?

Ach! Nobody told me St Petersburg was so cold. Good thing I have this trusty old coat.

I look like a homeless man in my coat. Aren't triple rehemmed lapels and molding leather tails cool anymore? Seriously.

This morning I walked out on/bumped into someone on/ got food on/entered a store on/made incessant references to Nevsky Prospect.

Alas, it's time for a new coat. I'm so static and terribly afraid of change, this could unwind my whole world!!

Saving for the coat will be a soul-crushing experience. I'm not allowed to eat 5/7 days.

Finally got my new threads today. Took it to work, I look Superfly. I'm not a gnat on a wall anymore, I'm Akaky 'Big Pimpin'' Akakyevitch.

Seriously, check out pics on my Flickr. This coat is so money, it doesn't even know how money it is.

Going to a party, can't wait to walk in all stately and proper with my new overcoat.

HOLY SHIT LET GO OF MY COAT!!!

OMG my coat is gone. Everything is ruined. </3 life.

I'm sick. The doctor says I'll be 'kaput' soon.

@BEYOND THE GRAVE
I'm dead and everyone's forgotten me, even those who have my coat. It's as though I never lived at all.

I'm a ghost. Will take my revenge and try to find my coat. Terrorize da po-po. They ain't got nothin' on me. Now where is my goddamn coat?

Secret Ops. Hit up the old mansion in an hour if anyone wants to help me rob this rich dude.

SUCCESS! Got his coat! Look at his face, he's totally shitting himself. LOL, Pwnd.

I feel so detached from my old self, as though I'm just a fraction of who I used to be.

I suppose I have what I want now, it's time to rest. If anyone sees my coat, tweet it.

The Old Man and the Sea
by Ernest Hemingway

@I_swear_I_don't_have_a_gun

Forty days since I have caught a fish. And . . .

The boy brings me the paper. We talk about baseball. I <3 DiMaggio.

I am a strange old man. Perhaps I will grow a beard.

I may have caught the big one.

It is pulling hard. The coast is far away. May be home late.

Still being pulled.

Still being pulled!

H.rd to 'et a sig--l out here. Dead zone. Dd t_is get thru?

The fish is a noble fish but I believe I have got him.

I have caught the fish, and he is grand

And I am bringing him back. Wait until you see this

And he is too big for the boat so I will have to pull him

And DiMaggio DiMaggio

And the sharks are coming

and they are eating the fish

and I have returned to Cuba and I have nothing to show

and the struggle has been valiant but I am unchanged
(except this beard I have grown)

and what can be said of my solitude for though it was
everything it came to nothing

Hmm. Perhaps this is a metaphor, perhaps this is life.

Perhaps I should kill myself one day.

The Inferno
by Dante Alighieri

@HolyHaha

I'm having a midlife crisis. Lost in the woods. Should have brought my iPhone.

I'm being attacked by three theoretical beasts! I don't think I'm in Italy any more!

Virgil found me. I'm not alone!

Wait. Virgil long dead. Hold on. Virgil sent by Beatrice. This is not Italy for sure.

Today, my lifelong idol says the only way to safety is to take a long, introspective journey through hell. FML.

Kicking it with Homer, Ovid, and Horace. Supergroup? World tour?

Big red demon wrapping his cock around himself. What the hell?

All of my Italian political enemies burning up down here. Called it!

A girl told me sex forgives no sexiness from the sexy. If anyone understands women, do tell.

I love Beatrice, but goddamn, after a talking tree, a tear-jerking encounter, and a mutant-dog, the lovin' better be worth it.

So this is embarrassing, but I started crying and Virgil smacked me and called me a big bitch. Grown men also cry, guys.

Met a guy who ate all his children and actually feels bad for HIMSELF. Creeped me out. Couldn't wait to say, 'Peace brotha, gotta split'.

I'm traveling toward Satan on the cold cracking trunks of ice. Frozen tears from crying eyes, no lies.

SATAN HAS THREE HEADS, AND THEY ARE TOTALLY EATING DUDES.

The best solution is to climb his big frozen ass. I'm still gonna die. *sighs* :(

MADE IT. SEE YOU NERDS LATER!

Beatrice shall soon make up for a lifetime of my desperate, torrid moods.

Gonna make looovvveeeeeee 2 ya girrrrrllll. DANTE OUT.

I have to climb a mountain now? You got to be kidding me. Is this a joke? Who the hell came up with this story? VIIIRRRGGGILLLLLLLLLLL!

A Hero of Our Time
by Mikhail Lermontov

@BAMF

My life will be of great consequence one day. Better keep a journal.

So here I am, in this small miserable resort. Me, an officer, with these fools. And best of all, they all love me. They adore me.

And yet, I'm a true monster, a truly sinister man, the worst of them all. I'm like a Russian Voldemort minus Rasputin.

My old friend Grushinsky is here. Friend, ha! I have none. He thinks I am his friend. Little does he know I am compelled to harm him.

Who is that sublime woman? She is perfect. Oh, excellent: Grushinsky seems to like her. I'm going to cock-block him. How typically me.

My plan to seduce her is simple: act like I always have better things to do, insult her, and act as though I have nothing left to live for.

Apparently she's begging for an introduction? I wonder if this kind of thing works in real life?

Mary is smart and beautiful, and totally wants my seed. But she doesn't know a thing about Byron. What an idiot.

I saw my former lover at the fountain. She's married. I didn't care about her until I heard that, then she became important again.

But this other girl is important too, kind of, I think. Maybe I just like c-blocking dudes. I'm an asshole, aren't I?

Grushinsky made a fool of himself in front of the girl. Now he has challenged me to a duel. Its OK, I'm always ready to die.

Mary is totally in love with me. I guess I have to pretend to be in love with her as well.

That's what one does, right? Even if I don't love her, and only plan on hurting her?

Shot Grushinsky without mercy. I don't feel bad about it. Mary is leaving. NOW she can't stand to see me? Not sure why.

My former lover is gone, too. But she's the one I love! Always now and forever. She's gone and I need her. Seems iffy but I am convinced!

That's it, I'm riding after her down the road.

Can't find her anywhere. All I want to do is sit by the side of this road and cry. I'm a devil, I'm Satan, and I'm crying.

I guess it's time to go back to the army, fall in love again, screw up some more marriages, ruin some more lives.

It's funny how people love me, can't get enough of me, are magnetically attracted to me, but can't stand me – and neither can I? What a life.

Beowulf

@Eazy-B

Just swam a whole river to settle a bet. Won, of course. Now this guy must sit on my horned helmet. A bet's a bet.

A faraway nation has a monster they want me to kill. They better have good wine so I can get crunk! Diet Sprite is also good.

What a bad ass monster. He likes to eat dudes' heads. Heads! That's intense. Ah, fuck it; I'll deal in the morning. I've gotta crash.

Next morning: HOLY LOKI! He's eating my companions, and not just their heads.

Quick psych eval: I'd blame his mother for naming him Grendel? Give me my broadsword and axe so I may slay this ugly prick.

Nasty fight. He kept trying to block my axe with his face – now he looks like Mickey Rourke.

Before I took Grendel out my men sodomized him, and I shat on his face. We used to do that in school, remember? (Is that messed up?)

@Grendellocks: Bah. That was way too easy. You're so dead that you can't even read this tweet. Fairy.

CELEBRATION TIME!!!! I saved the town and now I get to deflower all their virgins. But first . . .

Yawn. Speeches, speeches, speeches – they're never going to end! I believe I just had another birthday. What happened to half the virgins?

Uh oh. Grendel's mom showed up. She is really pissed. Wait, wait. Monsters have feelings?

This is the thing about moms: they're always scary whether you knocked up their daughter or killed their monster son.

Oh man: she just ate a dude in ONE BITE. A big dude. Not sure about the culinary appeal of human flesh. Maybe I should try it? Nah.

My sword is useless against her motherhood. A light-saber would make life much easier right about now.

Yes! Caught her off guard. Captured her! Let's make her eat her son's body? Is that messed up? We did that in school too . . .

More partying. But now I have to go back to my wife, Helga. She's got hairy legs, never trims down there, and refuses to let me get on top.

I just want to grow old and live out the remainder of my days in this garden, resting on my florals. Get it?

Just got a note. I have to kill a dragon. Can't they leave me alone? Why do Vikings have to fight monsters, but nobody else? Not fair.

I met the dragon, but my sword was ineffective. I failed everyone's expectations and suffered a fatal wound. I'm also king. Ugh.

I wish I had an heir, but sadly, my, uh, sword has failed me a third time.

Candide
by Voltaire

@MoYoLawn

If you try to bang your boss's daughter do you get canned? Hey, she came on to me. What is sex anyway? I'm clueless? And exiled.

Pangloss got exiled too. He's a deviant, exposing himself to people, sleeping with the maids. So that's what experimental bio means?

There's death everywhere, women with missing breasts, open bodies, shit on their faces. Isn't this world great? It's the best. The very best.

The Portuguese Inquisition wants to burn me as a sacrifice to the gods. What do they think I am, a Jew?

Time to go to South America. Do you think there are wireless hot spots in Eldorado?

Eldorado sucked. Who thought that Paradise would be so miserable? Plus, my girl isn't there, and there's no Paradise without the goils.

We've acquired two new people – Martin, a pessimist, and Cacambo, a black man–slave.

Pangloss has syphilis. He's all deformed. It's sad, but then you look at him and it's really fuckin' LOL.

I found the love of my life in Europe. She was forced into a prostitution ring. White slave trade. Real Lifetime Channel stuff. Tragic.

Crap. She's old and saggy, and used by the world. I don't wanna hit that, but I still love her, so I guess I will. I guess? Do I have to?

Ever wonder how we get across the world so quickly in this book? Continental flies six times daily from Eldorado to Paris.

Pangloss tells me the world is fine. Martin says it blows. Talk about conflicting viewpoints.

@Pangloss, @Martin: What matters is that life is OK and we just have to tend to our gardens. So STFU and tend, guys.

BTW, did you get the three garden metaphors throughout my story? Beginning, Eldorado, and the End?

Also, my girl hasn't shaved in years. Now that's a garden I really gotta tend to. Garden party!

Doctor Faustus
by Christopher Marlowe

@HighwayToHell

Science has begun to bore me. Why study it anymore? It's all facts and figures, nothing that really stirs the soul, you dig?

I know: I'll study evil instead. The occult. Sounds pretty rogue, nay?

OH WOW! A DEMON. First try, pretty sweet. Seems I'm a very efficient witch doctor.

Whoa! So Satan just walked in and said: 'Faustus, have I got a deal for you. Take it or leave it, but it's a once in a lifetime thing!'

Jesus. This contract is so hardcore and ironclad that Houdini couldn't escape. But Satan came back and made an offer I can't refuse.

I had to carve some stuff into my arm, and that kind of sucked. But as Rocky says, no pain, no gain.

Now I get to kick it with this demon. Some men have dogs, I have a demon. Upside: he has opposable thumbs, and magic.

@JustCallMeMrM: Alright, let's go do some damage. You have the costumes, I'll bring the vodka.

Running around causing problems is way better than science. When women ask what I do, I tell them I live dangerously. Literally.

I also say I have a one-way ticket to hell. Guess what that does to their panties? They disappear. No demon magic necessary! Sweet.

All this havoc has made me tired. I'm old and sick. I think I'm dying. Now what?

D DevilDog: Can I get out of the contract if I let you keep the deposit?

Shit. I should have seen this coming. Buyer's remorse! Buyer's remorse!

I never thought: 'Faustus, at the end of your life, this is going to bite you in the ass.' That's what living in the moment gets you.

Didn't someone make a whole wager about this sort of thing?

This is it. I'm falling into the abyss. The dark void of hell is swallowing me. Satan has come to take me! Need a little magic now.

What an allegory! If only part of the deal was that I'd learned how to rock and roll real good on the guitar.

Emma
by Jane Austen

@DarcyLover1815

Have you ever convinced a good friend that they should take affection to another, but then the gentleman does truly lust after you instead?

Perhaps I had better stop making matches. I tend to soil them royally. I really have a poor sense of people and reality.

Jane is coming to town! I hate that bitch. Unsure of the cause. I shall assume a kindly disposition. Still, I hate that skank.

Aha! Knew it. She's just as bad as I thought. Knightley says I'm jealous. I'M NOT JEALOUS!

Frank Churchill coming to visit also. I can't wait to meet him. I hear we'd make a splendid couple. Great news. I never want to get married.

The Churchill boy is fine. He totally wants me. I would get on that if I had any interest in him, but I certainly do not.

I love spending time with Frank. I do hope he wants to marry me. That would be so nice. Shame, I never want to get married.

Frank is leaving. I'll really miss him. I guess I love him. A little. Not enough to marry him, though.

No. No marriage. Not for me. I don't want that. Definitely. Did I say I'm not interested? Good. He's nothing to me.

- -

Frank is coming back!!!!!!! My heart swoons and dances at the notion! It's too bad I never want to get married.

- -

There was a ball last night. Frank and I were grinding it every which way. Shawty got lo lo lo lo.

- -

Why is Frank spending so much time with Jane? When I ask he insists nothing is happening.

- -

@Frankfurtive: Do you promise she's just a friend? Do you? Promise? Not that I care . . .

- -

How come I got so hot and sticky under my petticoat when I danced with Knightley? Probably best not to think about it.

- -

I don't love Frank. I should set him up with Jane even though they're just friends.

- -

Jane and Frank were together all along? Who saw that one coming? Good thing I was never interested. Not in the least.

- -

You, you've got what I need, but you say she's just a friend, you say she's just a friend . . .

- -

The only way to take care of Knightley is to marry him.

- -

Isn't it funny how I'm always thinking about things I seem not to care about, people I don't love, and marriages I don't want to have?

- -

Ender's Game
by Orson Scott Card

@BattleFool

School is great. Though we face alien threats, Earth is at peace. But one kid won't stop making fun of me.

Also, my older brother is a megalomaniacal sociopath who tortures me. And I want to have sex with my sister.

Otherwise my childhood development is balanced and will lead me to psychological normalcy in later life.

Got into a fight with that kid from school. The cops took me away, but instead of jail, I'm going into space. WTF?

It's a military school. I fight nonstop zero-gravity battles all day. Like laser-tag, only soul-crushing conflicts that kill my innocence.

Why do people always pick on me? Everyone knows I'm the best and the smartest. I invented a new fighting technique my FIRST DAY.

I was playing this cool video game when suddenly it busted out pics of my brother – and I died. As if I'm not stressed enough already.

In charge of my own army. Haven't lost a battle yet. One kid wants to kill me. How does this teach me how to fight aliens?

At times I feel inadequate but then realize I'm doing pretty well for an eight-year-old with a murder in my past and an army at my command.

The battles aren't fair. My army is a cohesive unit of lifelong friends, but I'm having a breakdown. Plus I miss my sexy sister.

Seriously, what did Kurt Vonnegut mean, 'We were just babies'? Excuse me, my BALLS HAVEN'T EVEN DROPPED YET and I have to save the world!

Flew over the cuckoo's nest. Live by a lake. Military tolerates my bs. Must be pretty desperate to entrust humanity's future to a child.

On to Command School. They say I'm ready to lead the entire human fleet against the bug-aliens. I thought I'd hit puberty first. Guess not.

An old Jew says he can teach me to defeat the aliens. Yeah right. This I know: no one older than eleven can be trusted to fight these days.

All my old friends are here! It's a great reunion. We're all training together.

The training keeps getting harder, and everyone seems so anxious. I wonder what it'll be like to fight the REAL war?

Final exam day. Everyone's so anxious. The Old Jew says I'll battle him today. But he's not at a computer. Now I'm really anxious.

Has anyone ever committed genocide by accident? Long story short: there goes my sanity. Finally. Thanks, military–industrial complex.

The only way to repent for my crime is to tell the aliens' story. I will become the tweeter for the dead. Also, I finally hit puberty.

Great Expectations
by Charles Dickens

@piMp

My sister is such a bitch! And her husband, talk about pussy-whipped. I'm going out on the marshes. I hate this place.

The walk was a bad idea. I met a prisoner who demanded bread and a file. He looks like a pederast. And a murderer. Amber alert?

I have to sit in the crazy woman's house. She lives in the basement, sits in the same clothes. Her fiancé really dodged a bullet there.

Her granddaughter Estella is pretty hot. She's ten. I'm ten, too. All she does is make fun of me. Maybe it's my name.

I whupped a kid in the garden. He wanted to box, so I boxed his head. Float like a butterfly, sting like a bee. Taught Sonny Liston a lesson.

I'm an adult now. Someone left a huge wad of cash in my name. Do I hear London calling the faraway towns?

Remember that kid I beat up? He's my roommate, and get this, he says HE won the fight. Mhm, yeah, right, both he and George Foreman.

Kids here are all assholes. Odd, but I slowly feel myself becoming a snob. Maybe it's the tweed jacket?

I think that old woman in the basement left me the money. I ran into her granddaughter last night. Maybe she'll show me some ankle.

My roommate is a drag. He keeps ankle-blocking me. I'll have a talk with him; 'Bro, I'm trying to get the anger-bang on this girl, GTFO.'

My sister's husband came to visit. What a classless country-swine. Doesn't even know how to tie a proper cravat.

Estella keeps hanging around with other gentledudes. My heart . . . hurts . . . is this what they call love?

Shes a coquette, a flirt. I can't tell who she likes. I can't predict what's coming next! What am I dealing with?

Heavens. My financial benefactor was the criminal. The murdering pederast from the beginning. Glad I canceled the alert.

I'm starting to forget my roots. I'm an asshole.

I'm in my old town with a crazy Gollum-like guy following me. I wanna throw a rock at him, but I think that's assault. Anyone pre-law?

Estella is staying in her grandma's castle. That family is action-packed with issues. Like grandma like granddaughter.

I love her, but if she's sitting alone in a castle there's something wrong with the girl. I don't want to marry Sylvia Plath over here.

Heart of Darkness
by Joseph Conrad

@JungleFever

Did you know that back in the day Romans traveled along the Thames in wooden rowboats? Crazy, huh?

Out of work again – economy is tough. My aunt says she can get me a job, but it's so embarrassing accepting help from women.

Women really are naïve! Can you imagine if they were allowed to run the world? Disaster! Luckily that'll never happen in good old England.

Heading down to Africa on a boat. Too hot! I get the creeping sense this job isn't going to be as cushy as they made it sound.

The natives seem unhappy. Some are even violent! Why don't they appreciate how much we've done for them? Ungrateful welfare leeches, I say!

Boat's broken. Stuck at camp. These bureaucrats are turds. Whole operation is an oppressive disaster. I don't want to talk to anybody.

Keep hearing about this 'unorthodox' Kurtz guy. Sounds interesting. Probably never overtweets about trivialities. My kind of man.

Boat fixed. Time to find out what Kurtz is up to. Hope 'unorthodox methods' doesn't mean buggery. Or worse – if that's possible.

NATIVES THROWING SHIT AT ME. CUT IT OUT!

Doc says that spending time with black savages makes your brain shrink. Oh well.

Consumed by Jungle. Madness seeps into me. Must find Kurtz before I lose my mind to overwhelming terror. This isn't Disney's jungle ride.

Found Kurtz. He rules the natives as king. Took one as a wife. His madness is a new mental condition. Let's call it 'jungle fever'. ROFL.

Kurtz dead. His lover abandoned him. I oversaw his death. Last words either 'the horror' or that his woman was 'a whore'. Hard to tell.

Back in Europe. Feel as if I look forever into that immense heart of . . . what? Shadows? Night? Gloom? Something pitch black?

Must see Kurtz's fiancée. Ugh, the lack of women in Africa has spoiled me.

She demands to know his last words. But women are too stupid to know the truth. Must she be lied to? Help me out.

@Betrothed: He said . . . your name. Isn't that nice? That's how the world works: like a cute, predictable love story. Are you happy now?

So about the Thames: I can get a boat. Anyone up for a quick pleasure cruise?

King Lear
by William Shakespeare

@HiLEARious

Look upon how much my daughters do loveth me. One day this kingdom will all be theirsth!

What? Cordelia loves me only as much as she should? What effrontery! For that she'll get naught. Nada. Zip.

King of France took Cordelia. 'Love' or somesuch – as if she knows what that is! Luckily, Goneril and Regan love dear old Dad.

Alright, I'm leaving, and taking a crew with me. Me and my boyz will be fine. Just fine.

What, my ungrateful girls are kicking me out? I'll be cold and homeless. This sucketh. Very unexpected. Am I right?

Seriously. They SAID THEY LOVED ME. I really do not get it. Who lies just because they know it will win them land and power??

I guess compared to 'Ronald' and 'Gonorrhea', Cordelia wasn't so bad. What a Shakespearean twist of events!

They jail me, they betray me. I hear the French may come and put an end to this madness, though. Gloucester has it all worked out.

Ah! Spoke too soon. Gloucester's 'vile jelly' had to be removed. And by 'vile jelly' I mean his eyeballs.

Clearly the best possible solution is to run around naked on a hill in a thunderstorm. Goddamn, these winds do sorely rustle my privates.

Even if my heirs weren't evil, dividing a major nation into several arbitrary bordering factions is a pretty bad idea to begin with, huh?

This infighting has become vicious. @Kent, @Edmund, @Albany: Quit this! Too much intrigue for a confused old man!

Cordelia and I captured by Edmund. This is the part where we get rescued, right?

Cordelia is very weak, but yet the feather stirs – she lives!

Nix that – Cordelia dead :(

I am overcome with grief. Other two daughters also dead. Well, don't REALLY care. A great turn-around from earlier! A Dickensian twist, no?

Everyone's managed to kill off each other. Now Albany thinks I should retake the throne, but I feel so very very tired . . .

Lysistrata
by Aristophanes

@PussyWhip

- -

This war is just too absurd. We can't go on this way.

- -

What's something we can leverage against men? What's the one thing we're good for again? It's on the tip of my tongue . . .

- -

@WomynOfGreece: No sleeping with your husbands until they agree not to fight anymore.

- -

This should work well. After all, you come home from the war, all you want is a beer and blow job. Imagine if you could only have a beer?

- -

@WomynOfGreece: If they force you, remember, no legs to the ceiling. NO ORGASMS. That gives them the power. And we can't have that now can we?

- -

@WomynOfGreece: You also have to give up the Lioness on the Cheese Grater. I know it's great, but lay off it for a bit.

- -

Men are back. Storm the Acropolis!!! We can have a sit-in. Or a lock-down. Like a sitting pussy lock-down.

- -

We shouldn't stay at the Acropolis together too long though. We might get on the same cycle. That would mean a mess for the sit-in.

- -

You think men at war have it bad, we just sit here, waiting to service them. Then they leave for a decade. And batteries not invented yet.

- -

Talk about hit-and-quit. Then I have to raise yo' baby!

Our men are going nuts. It's really working. They're horny as hell – and no war in sight.

Let's see if we can get them to agree to some absurd shit. Maybe they'll let us vote, have jobs, own property. Equal rights win, perhaps?

Let's piss them off even more and lock ourselves in the Acropolis again.

Can you believe that they're already getting some peace-contracts ready? What men won't do for sex . . . Jeez.

Time to overcome our differences and just get it on. Sexual healing sounds good? Right now! Thank Athena, I feel so hollow.

Whooooo, party in the Acropolis!!! We're going streaking through the forum and into the temple!!!

After all, we really just want some action. If we fought wars and men came up with this plan, peace would have come much sooner . . .

In Cold Blood
by Truman Capote

@PerrySmith

- -

Dick and I off to rob some rich farmers. I don't care to
do it so much, but Dick insists and I usually just listen
to him.

- -

Uh oh. Farmers had no money so I shot them point blank
with a shotgun. I can't help it. Mother didn't love me, so I
have to kill people.

- -

(Sometimes I just want to go to Mexico and hunt treasure
in the ocean. I'm not a total failure; I have dreams and
aspirations!)

@ClutteredReporting
Big news! Gentle family of four murdered in small Kansas
town! Seems like a good opportunity for some reporting.
#bignews #crime #mycareer

- -

@PerrySmith
On the run. Dick conning us all the money we need. He's
so powerful and in control. Even though he's illiterate, I
am . . . drawn to his manliness.

- -

I have this dream where a giant bird kills all the mean
people who make me murder families. Wish a giant bird
would come save me IRL.

- -

Got picked up by the law. Why won't The Man just leave
me alone?? Can't they see I'm real educated, and Dick is
the stupid criminal?

- -

@ClutteredReporting
My Southern background and career as a New York literary homosexual will no doubt win me the trust and favor of these Midwestern farmers.

@PerrySmith
In prison. This nice man from New York wants to know my story – think he will help me go free by telling my side.

I guess the Clutters were actually a nice family, and their death has wounded this town and the police who investigated the crime.

But really, I wish a giant bird would just kill them and carry me off to paradise.

Sentenced to death. When's the reporter going to finish his book?? A lot of weird people on death row.

Out of appeals. Hurry up with that book! Dear Truman Capote, it's really not fair, everyone here has a social disease!

Ah well – too late! Sorry to everybody, I guess. Honestly, I can't decide much of anything for myself. Maybe that was my problem?

@ClutteredReporting
Famous! Book a big hit with everyone except all those involved. End is a bit gruesome though, maybe add a sentimental scene at a graveyard.

A shame this book has lost me all of my friends. If only I was less obsessed with work I wouldn't be so alone, so terribly fat and alone.

Made some new friends. Answer to my prayers. I had to promise I'd never write about them. I can live with that.

Medea
by Euripides

@GoldenFarce

Finally moved into the new place. Jason can find a respectable job, I'll stay home and raise the kids. Life is finally looking up!

Seems 'respectable job' means screwing the king's daughter. Not cool. Need to consult my girlfriends.

Good, the gals stand outside my house all the time. The constant chanting is creepy, but all agree: Jason crossing the line!

When he gets home we'll talk. I'm sure we can work it out. But what's the best way to approach this? Any advice, anyone? #wackrelationships

He says he 'has to' marry her because we're 'wanted criminals' and we need 'protection'. Yelled at him. Lots. He doesn't listen!

Checked Kosmo, but all hot Spartan sex tips, no advice for what to do when refugee husband marries another woman because he *loves you*.

I feel a bit of the LOCO coming on! Mood swings and witchcraft: two things every femme fatale needs.

D Jason: Hey baby, come home. I made a gift for your wedding. I ain't mad anymore baby, I promise.

LOL, he totally bought it. Yeah, it's a nice dress – with POISON. Isn't that funny? My girlfriends don't think so. They're weirded out.

D KingOfAthens: Can I crash at your place? Please? Promise, or I'll kill you with my magic just like I killed the king of Corinth.

Can't. Stand. The. Chanting. Why do I always get the chorus of criticism?! Some friends!!

Uh-oh. Jason is home and he's pissed.

Ran inside with a sword before Jason could stop me. Didn't want the kids to hear us arguing, so I took them to a better place – the freezer.

Jason very unhappy I murdered the children. Told him to go bury HIS WIFE! I thought it was a great comeback but it didn't help.

Dad sent me some dragons. I'm gone. Jason can deal with his own shit. I'm off to Athens. Maybe THEY can handle an independent woman!

I swear I'm not crazy, I'm just passionate. I just want respect. I just want to be loved . . .

Nineteen Eighty-Four
by George Orwell

@Ratatouille

London is a totally ridiculous place these days. (I actually mean ridiculous in a totalitarian way. Best keep this to myself.)

What's with slogans like 'War Is Peace'? Do only I see they make no sense? Seems someone in government is on a very big opposites kick.

I found a little journal and a tiny place in my room where Big Brother ISN'T watching. Now I can record my dissident thoughts/jerk it.

Look, brother, if I wanted to be WATCHED doing my dirty business, I'd make a sex tape. Oh? You already have it?

God I hate rats. It's important that you know how much I hate rats, because I really, really hate rats.

At work; dullsville. How can rewriting history be fun if you're betraying the timeless ideal of truth? Let's see: Truth Is Lies?

Disregard last tweet. Need to keep those bad thoughts out of my head, otherwise I'll have to make a trip to the Ministry of Love.

P.S. By 'Love' they mean imprisonment, execution, and unspeakable torture. In that order. Like I said, opposites are the new white.

Met a drab hot girl today. Slipped me a note saying she loved me. Romance is forbidden because everything good in this society is bad. Hmm.

Fuck it, life's a risk. Had sex on the hillside; went wild, though for a moment I was ashamed of my varicose veins.

While you should never date a hooker or a porn star, I suggest a girl who writes porno. Guess what she thinks about all day?

We defeated Eurasia in the war! Or was it Eastasia all along? Either way, we'll take them as usual!

Julia and I do it every day. Nice store owner rented us a room without cameras. Must not launder bed sheets too often or we'll be caught.

My boss wants to see me; this can't be good. Maybe I'll get laid off and have to transfer to the Ministry of Irony.

Surprise. He is part of a secret organization devoted to overthrowing the party. Julia and I are in. This is so exciting!

Just kidding. Big Brother WAS watching! Carted off to the Ministry of Love, as I tweet. Makes me think of childhood, for some reason.

Sometimes you're locked up in a secret government prison. Then you meet this crazy old woman. And it's your mother.

Hard to post through endless rounds of torture. O'Brien tells me that the Party wants power for power's sake. Deep, man.

DAMNIT. FUCKING RATS IN MY FUCKING FACE. WHY DID I TELL I HATE RATS? NO KILL JULIA PLEASE GODDAMNIT. FORGOT: THERE'S NO GOD.

I'm a free man. I do love Big Brother. He is doubleplusgood – truly, in my heart, I love him. Because I am free. So very free.

On the Road
by Jack Kerouac

@Didn'tTypeOnTP!

For TWITTERATURE of *On the Road* by Jack Kerouac, please see *On the Road* by Jack Kerouac.

Notes from Underground
by Fyodor Dostoevsky

@TweetsFromUndergrnd

I'm a sick man. A very sick man. My liver hurts. Good. I'm sure the doctor could fix it, but I ruin my liver to spite my face.

I used to be a magistrate. No big deal. Mostly just teeth-gnashing and yelling at officers. Typical bureaucratic nonsense.

I know how math works, and I know 2x2=4. But it would be fucking wild if 2x2=5, eh? And after all, why shouldn't it?

My life is so stagnant, but I just love sitting on the couch all day. Inaction: where the living is easy. If you can call it living.

Oh my tooth! Oh my awful tooth. LISTEN TO ME: My tooth hurts and my wailing will cause you pain, too. Hah!

I want revenge on all those who have harmed me. Is this unhealthy? Good. I'm a bit of a sociopath, aren't I?

An officer pushed me at a bar. I will find this *pizda* son of a bitch and maybe murder him slowly. I'm a bit of a sociopath, aren't I?

I always walk on Nevsky, trying to find him. If I see him, I'll challenge him to a duel. Because it's the rational thing to do.

Yes, the best thing to do is bump into him.

Bump. That *ebanatyi pidaraz* didn't even notice!! God, I'm an insignificant *khuy*, oh well.

I'm going out to dinner with some people. I don't really want to. But I want to go to prove that I can. Maybe I can ruin the evening.

I'm waiting, they're not here yet. It's been an hour. Couldn't they call? *Dolboebs.*

Alright, they're here now. I shouldn't have drunk all that wine. No biggie. I'm only six glasses ahead.

Can you believe one of these idiots tried to talk about Shakespeare? What could he know about Shakespeare? *Blyadischa!*

Speaking of *blyadischa*, we're going to a brothel. This should be fun. I love hookers.

I met this sweet girl Liza. I did her, made fun of her, convinced her life as a whore was crap, then split. I'm a bit of a sociopath, no?

I also told her she could come to my house if she wanted to escape. Ohh, the crazy things I say during sex.

Now I have to borrow money from my friends for this hooker. Sex may be God's gift but it's not cheap.

Liza actually showed up at my house. I yelled at her and made her cry. She left.

I chased after her for a bit but couldn't find her. My life is miserable and lonely. I should get my sociopath shit together.

Of Mice and Men
by John Steinbeck

@IAmWithSam

Nothing beats hanging out with a ret— . . . idiot, all day.
How did I become a babysitter for Rain Man? Minus the
superhuman talent, that is.

Lennie killed some mice. Great. It's kind of ironic, because
compared to a smart guy like me, he's kind of a mouse,
isn't he?

Come to think of it, it is pretty funny, because, you know, I
am a MAN, and they are MICE, and Lennie is KIND OF
BOTH. Get it? (Obvious?)

Need to find work. Ret— . . . Lennie here doesn't know
how to monitor his food intake – we're running out of
DOUGH. Bam! Pun!

Do they call it the Great Depression because everybody is
depressed?

We found a ranch to work at. Lennie none too bright, but
good with his hands. Real steady hands. I'd trust him
handling just about anything.

Playing cards all day. The rancher's son is an asshole, but
his wife is a pretty swell gal. Also a bit of a party girl.

@Lennie: Goddamnit: don't you know groping women is illegal? it's 1929, man, women have RIGHTS now. They're EQUAL. Kind of.

- -

Now Lennie's in trouble with the law. How can you accuse a guy of rape when he doesn't know his boner from a hole in the ground?

- -

There's a pretty cool guy here – @Candy. You should check him out, though Candy is kind of a stripper name, isn't it?

- -

Lennie broke the owner's son's hand, which was kind of funny because his bones popped out of his hand. They were, like, visible!

- -

Lennie just wants to live off the fat of the land. Working like a dog in a rock and roll band.

- -

Lennie came back into the cabin with that look on his face and I said, Lennie, did you kill another woman?

- -

He told me he had done it again, he thought. Why do I get stuck with the dangerously disabled? Did Forrest Gump ever hurt anyone?

- -

I hear the lynch mob outside. This is the third time this year that we gotta go 'cause Lennie made a mess of things.

- -

I can't deal with this shit anymore. I have a headache, I need an Advil and a good roll in the hay. But Lennie is the Anti-Poon.

- -

I'm going do what I shoulda long ago: shoot this ret— . . . friend, in the head. Otherwise, the mob will torture him. He deserves a quick death.

He is my friend though. But I have to do it myself; the law won't euthanize the disabled here, and Texas is way too far away.

Another day in the good old Depression.

What America needs now is a bottle of Prozac.

Robinson Crusoe
by Daniel Defoe

@ImNotGilligan

What does my dad know? Embarking on a sea-journey as an indentured servant seems like a perfectly wonderful idea.

Man-of-war screwed us. I'm a slave. What a fright it gave me! Oh well, life has its lulz and downs.

I tossed this other slave from the fishing boat, and I'm off to Africa with a slave boy.

I really do like this slave boy, he's like family, a really good friend, sticking by me through thick and thin. I'll always be loyal to him.

I sold the slave boy to a Captain who offered to take me to South America. I'll use the rest of the money to buy some tobacco.

I'm finally going to be a sailor! Someone's taking me on their ship.

Jesus Christ. A storm! We're sinking!! Wait, wait. Here's a great idea: If I live I'll be forever loyal to God.

Faith shmaith: How could an inexperienced farmer-slave-runaway survive when the professional sailors drowned?

Hmm. No, I think it's best to become really religious – and then raid the boat for everything that's inside it.

The best possible solution now is to make a pro and con list about the island. Pro: I'm not dead. Con: I might as well be.

- -

Incredible. Everything one might EVER need to survive on an island was in that ship. Guns, food, bread, books, you name it.

- -

What if there are cannibals on the island? No, probably not. But what if there are? Nah, there ain't . . . SHIT. A FOOTPRINT. CANNIBALS!

- -

Here's what's odd: I've been here so many years and haven't thought about pussy once. Go ahead, call me introspective.

- -

You'd think in a diary about solitude I'd write something emotional, but nah, that'd be so emo. I'm not in the mood.

- -

I've rescued a cannibal. I'll call him Friday, because after all this time I still know what day it is, and can't think of anything better.

- -

Friday, you shall be my slave, you owe me your life. Do what I say. Don't bite me. Aren't you glad I found you?

- -

Hey, more people on the island. Let's party! Who's got the rum? I should open a bar, call it Islands!!!

- -

DRUNNNNNKKKKKKK! Beach limbo!

- -

I'm preparing to attack a pack of wolves. I haven't seen wolves in thirty years, now there's a billion. Maybe I'm still drunk.

- -

Ahoy. A pirate ship comes to rescue me. What, the editors want a sequel? I guess it's time to go to Asia.

- -

Romeo and Juliet
by William Shakespeare

@DefNotAHomeo

@JulieBaby

My family won't stop fighting the Capulets. Life should be a party. Make love, not war!

Here comes my benevolent cousin Mercutio.

Ah, how I love women! No, not that OLD woman. A new woman. I shall have no fun at this party, thinking of this woman I love . . .

But the crew 'tis in want of drink. We must crash this ball!

WTF is Mercutio talking about? Everyone knows fairies don't exist! Whoa. Hot babe cometh near. Must try the uninvited grind.

She totally digs it! Ah, sin! Sin again! I'm such a wit, and such a pimp.

Uh-oh. She's a Capulet. Methinks this can go nowhere good, but why stop now?

Later: Maybe if I stick around I can get a glimpse of her titties through the window.

D DefNotAHomeo: Psst. Wherefore art thou?

D JulieBaby: What do you mean 'where am I'? I'm right under the balcony! Does no one understand English anymore?

Her nurse asketh if I want to marry Juliet. She is the sun but this is waaay too fast. Am I being punk'd? Where's Ashton?

D Tybalt: Why are you hitting me? I can barely direct message the question with your sword up my ass.

Mercutio, you horse dropping. Why'd you have to die? @PrinceofCats: One of us is joining him . . . NOT IT!

Sometimes you kill your wife's cousin in a duel, and then you have to go to Mantua to hide out. Yeah, life sucks.

What? Juliet is dead? No. Orders to kill me on the spot? No! Curse the stars that led me to believe in Hollywood endings!

I have my poison, will return to Verona, take care of business.

Found fair Juliet. She's dead, and definitely not faking it! (Didn't move when I poked her there.) Alas, I must drink this terrible brew.

'O, I am fortune's fool!' Maybe just a tool. And so I die. BTW that other woman I was into before Juliet? Would've been a safer bet.

D DefNotAHomeo: Wake up, my love. C'mon. Fun's over. Wake up. Quit it! Not funny. Where's Ashton? Oh shit. Bottoms up.

@Montague, @Capulet: Can't we all just get along?

Anna Karenina
by Leo Tolstoy

@DoTheLocomotion

My sister-in-law wants to divorce my brother. I have to go to Moscow to stop that nonsense. Might as well party while I'm there.

Some gentleman danced with me the whole night. We got a little grinding on, but not too much. This is formal Russian society, mind you.

Apparently by dancing with Vronsky I pussy-blocked a girl called Kitty. I suppose that's ironic. You'd think with a name like that . . .

LOL, Kitty had a nervous breakdown and had to leave the country. Takes her out of the picture.

Is it irresponsible to start a pretty obvious love affair with Vronsky?

After all, my husband is a geezer. Do you know what it feels like to have old AARP balls on your face? I shudder at the thought.

My husband doesn't seem to mind as long as I don't make a fool of him in public. Talk about spineless. Maybe it's all the herniated discs.

Alexei Vronzarelli – da Vronz – is my lover now. I missed my period. I may be pregnant with his baby.

My husband caught us in the house. We weren't fucking, just playing Yahtzee, but still, I guess having him around was a bit inappropro.

My husband peaced. He says he can't 'deal with this whore'. I guess I'm too much woman for him.

I almost died giving birth. Boy, you never really consider what it's like popping an eight-pound thing out of you. It's really quite scary.

My husband returned when he heard the news. I told him he was a father. His eyes lit up. Then I told him the truth. He started crying, lol.

He has forgiven me for infidelity (and the tasteless joke) and has offered me a divorce. I kinda feel bad taking it though.

I decided I'm gonna treat him well, and not divorce him. Instead I'll continue cuckolding him. Yeah, that sounds better.

Whew! Glad I cleared my conscience on that one.

I'm moving in with Vronsky.

Life is so boring. Let's play a game to see how quickly the perfect married lover can turn into the girlfriend from hell.

HE'S CHEATING ON ME. I know it. He says he went to visit his mom. Yeah, sure, if by mother he means some WHORE.

His mother wants him to marry a princess. She says he shouldn't be living in sin with a married woman. Fuckin' in-laws.

I can't take this anymore. I'm going out to find him. If I find him in bed with his mother I'll be really pissed. I'm on my way.

Alright, twenty rubles says that I can toss my bag in the air, run across the tracks, and catch it before the train arriv—

This user's account has been deactivated.

Sherlock Holmes
by Sir Arthur Conan Doyle

@KeepDiggingWatson

Ah, sitting in my study on Baker Street. Wearing my new velvet dressing gown. Taking some, uh . . . snuff. What a relaxing evening.

Puffing the pipe. A pounding at the door. Go away. Woman in distress, crying. Watson terrorizing fair sex again? No. Perhaps a mystery.

Why do people ask me to solve their problems? Let me enjoy my high. Watson says it's a bad habit, but what does he know? I'm the detective.

I have to investigate a factory where this woman's lover was the foreman. She thinks the company's trying to knock him off.

Doing a few lines before I start the job. Can't solve a mystery without my miracle powder. By which I mean cocaine.

Asked clever questions. I could tell all were lying. No mention of the valuable metals hidden beneath the factory. Moriarty involved?

In the water closet doing a bump. Watson says I'm paranoid. Says the nose candy affects my work. Fine. Let him buy his own.

Continuing investigation. Made brilliant deductions on many snorts and very little evidence. Notice salt deposits on factory owner's brogues?

- -

Watson says I only THINK I'm smart because I'm high. Does that mean he's not gay, only thinks he is?

- -

Need opiates to restore calm. And another gram of Colombian marching powder. It's hard to be the River Phoenix of nineteenth-century England.

- -

Damsel came back; something afoot at the factory. Broke out the bushbait so I could wake up. She wants a hit. Elementary.

- -

We stripped off. I did lines off her tits. Couldn't get it up and know not why. Smoked an entire pouch of tobacco instead.

- -

A working girl in Staines gave me a clue about the factory owner. He's a regular customer. Pays in gold coin. High roller.

- -

Why are the lights at 221 Baker Street so damn bright in the morning? Why does Watson talk so loud? Elementary, my dear STFU!

- -

The foreman/lover discovered a precious metal. The salt deposits were cyanide crystals to poison people who got in the way. Like him.

- -

Note to self: Don't snort the crystals NO MATTER WHAT!

- -

Itch. Bugs in my skin. Need a line and a drink. Have the culprits poisoned me to keep me from foiling their dastardly plot? Nose bleeding.

- -

Decided to call in the bobbies because confronting criminals is scary. I just like books, long walks on the beach, and deductive reasoning, you know?

- -

Another case solved. I'm the Batman of Britain.

- -

Robert Downey Jr playing me in a film? Totally cool. Perfect.

- -

Eugene Onegin
by Alexander Pushkin

@MrDandyMan

Life is pretty boring when all you do is bag bitches, take names, and kick ass. Also I rock and roll all night. And every day.

Well almost as a magical cure for my boredom, my uncle is dead, and left me his house. Party in the countryside? I'll say.

There's a poet here, he's rather kind, I'm going to meet his family.

I always think the best way to get the ladies is to affect mystery and apathy.

His wife's sister is a bookworm, but wants me. I'm getting a clinger vibe from her. She would marry me in thirty seconds if I were into down.

I got a really awkward love letter from the bookworm sister while I was walking around town.

I'm not going to dignify this hussy with a response. I'll just scare the shit out of her in the street. Or I can shun her.

Do I *have* to see this girl again? She'll go *Fatal Attraction* on me. I'd rather have a concussion. Will she bother me, I wonder?

Everyone told me I was very polite, but condescending. How can you both be polite and condescend? Irony? Hypocrisy?

I've been invited to a ball by the poet. I dressed for three hours. It's a miserable time because it reminds me of the damned aristocracy!

I'm so furious. I wanted to leave society and here I am again! The poet and his party are awful. I'll torment him by flirting with his wife.

He left in a rage. I got the best of that engagement. Does this sort of manipulative, demonic behavior work in real life?

Wanna hear something really funny? I try to sleep with his wife, he challenges me to a duel, I shoot him and he dies!

No, seriously, pumped some lead into him, spilled that lyrical blood. I messed him up, no surprise!

The lunatic damsel who I turned down rifled through my documents and thinks I'm nothing but an amalgam of literary heroes!

This place is crap, I'm leaving. I probably shouldn't have shot the poet. Bad, bad news. I'm a wicked person. Woah!

Remember that girl who wanted me, the clinger? Well I met her again, and she got really fine. I was such a fool!

She says she can't love me just because she is married? Is she trying to gaslight me? What a tool.

- -

She gave me a whole speech, like the one I gave her, about why she can't sleep with me.

- -

Life kind of sucks, leave it to irony and selfishness to come back and bite me in the ass. I'm bored. Leave me be!

- -

The Crying of Lot 49
by Thomas Pynchon

@WASTEdEnergy

Been made executor of my ex-boyfriend's estate. I guess there's no such thing as a free gold-dig. Heading down to San Narciso tomorrow.

From hilltop, the city looks like a giant circuit board. I feel like this image might stick with me.

A circuit board is something that conveys information. Information seems like an important thing, but perhaps I'm missing something.

In the motel, watching bad TV movies with a lawyer. This is the most awkward seduction ever.

Taking a dump. Stall graffiti is weird: 'Jack was here' and 'the English Patient sucks'. Mysterious symbol of a worldwide conspiracy?

Anybody know what this W.A.S.T.E. thing is? There's also a picture of a horn that I think I once saw tattooed on a hipster's wrist.

These stamps sure do look funny.

Not really focusing on the whole executor thing. Too into the whole conspiracy. Hard to concentrate with this music always playing though.

Everyone around me has a funny name. I guess our parents' generation was big on wit. 'Genghis Cohen'? 'God'? 'Brad'? 'Britney'?

At the theater. The play also mentions the 'Tristero' thing. Talked to this dilettante director in the shower. He's totally DTF.

Trying to get information everywhere, but with little success. Talked to some guy about entropy. Will see a scientist about it.

Scientist a total creep! He tried to show me Maxwell's Semen, if you know what I mean.

Isn't it ironic how I am obsessed with finding information about a POSTAL conspiracy, which HAS TO DO WITH INFORMATION? That's so clever.

Back in SF. Husband is tripping balls. I say LSD isn't for me. Meanwhile, I'm going to wander around all night seeing the horn everywhere.

The more I investigate, the more information I seem to lose track of. That whole entropy thing, you know. God, my life is a clever one.

My analyst lost it. I guess even our civilization has its discontents. Pretty HILARIOUS!

Finally got estate inventoried. Auction in a couple of days. Somebody buying up the stamps that are key to this thing, but they won't meet us.

They changed their minds! Lot 49 to be bought IN PERSON. Finally the truth! Will tweet what I find out as soon as I lay my eyes on them . . .

The Epic of Gilgamesh

@UrukRockCity

It's pretty great being king: part human, part God, ALL ladies' man.

But I keep having terrible dreams. Are the Gods displeased with my arrogance? Not mine. Not possible. No way.

My approval rating's WAY down. Don't understand why most citizens feel 'fighting' and 'banging our wives' shouldn't be top royal priorities?

Must attend a wedding party. Wearing fly royal robes to properly perform my prima nocta duty. Ba-da-bing!

Why are a hooker and a big hairy dude named Enkidu blocking my way? He says he is stronger, and I'm a disgusting pervert. That hurts, man.

Kicked his ass. What he said about my debauchery struck a nerve, but we're buddies now. I'd even call him . . . my bro.

@EnkiduTheUruk: Scene is suddenly boring now that I'm reformed. You want to go slay a demon, bro?

Everyone says transgressing into a God's domain is a mistake. What do they know? Enkidu's got my back – let's do it.

Oh shit. Demons are way more terrifying in person. Managed to get his armor off with promises/lies of nonstop demon-loving groupies.

I was going to spare the demon's life, but Enkidu had me take him out. Ruthless. Perhaps all that hair itches.

As suspected: all the ladies want to get it on now that I've slain the demon. But I must decline. I'm a clean man these days.

I just can't win with women. Before, nailing all the ladies was bad. Now I refuse to seduce, and the Gods send a giant bull to kill me?

Killed the bull, too. Is there any fight I can't win? Enkidu seems nervous now. He says the Gods will be even more pissed.

Great. That's it. I'm leaving Uruk. My best friend in the world is dead, all because the Gods couldn't handle our great bromance.

Found another great hero. He survived the flood of many days and nights that wiped out humanity. There's a story I've never heard before.

I wonder if he can be my new friend. I need a new heroic friend. I just feel so . . . lonely.

He says I have to stay awake for seven days to impress him. Why can't I just slay another demon? Killing things is so much easier.

I've failed. Headed home. Life not the same without my Enkidu. There will never be another like him. The greatest bromance of my life.

The Odyssey
by Homer

@IthacaOnMyMind

Dawn and her rose–red fingers fingered herself. Another morning! God, this island is terrible.

Calypso wanted to marry me. Bitch. Who does she think I am? I have a wife! Thank the Gods for allowing my escape.

We landed on an island. Found a cave filled with food. How convenient.

Uh oh. This cave is a giant's lair. He has a taste for cheese, and my companions. He also has only one eye. Trying to keep from laughing.

Got him drunk. Put a hot poker in his ONE EYE when he blacked out. That will show him - if he could see. LOL. Time to leave.

Damn. Poseidon pissed. How was I supposed to know One–Eye was his son? What Olympian whore did he sleep with to get an issue like that?

Escaped again. Found another island. Some hot babes up ahead. I'm married but it's been years. Can't hurt. A guy needs to get his freak on.

Circe a nut job. Time to go, but the boat is broken. Can't afford AAA tow. I'll push it. Circe turned my men into pigs. PIGS. Had a laugh.

On the road/sea again. Heard about some sea monsters up by Sicily? Anybody else hear about this?

@TheTemptations: Nice song girls, but we can't stop!
@MyMen: Tie me tighter, hurry!

Found sea monster: a billion-headed fucker who totally trashed my ship and killed all the crew. Getting sucked into a whirlpool now. Sigh.

So I'm passed out after the accident, lying naked on some rock, and this girl shows up.

Talk about embarrassing, this is worse than when we caught Achilles with his . . . cousin.

These guys can help me, but their wine is MAAAAD strong. I haven't been this trashed since Junior Prom.

Finally home. Everything good! Wait, who the fuck are these dudes hitting on Penelope?

@Suitors: You have defiled my house, dishonored the gods, and tried to seduce my wife. TIME TO TASTE MY BLUE STEEL.

Got my lady back thanks to the weird decorating we did. My son is now a man and not a sniveling bitch. All is well. Gosh I am a clever man!

The Picture of Dorian Gray
by Oscar Wilde

@MajorLeagueAesthole

Ah, the light of innocence! My young life! My dear friend Basil wishes to paint me. Ah, but I am so pretty.

Portrait done, but Basil says I cannot see it. Too much of him in it.

I've met his friend Lord Henry. He arranged for me to have the portrait. He seems like a good man.

Spending my days with Lord Henry. He has taught me wit and how to appreciate beauty. This can only improve my life, right?

Sadly my beauty will one day cease. Perhaps I could preserve it by having the doc pull and staple the skin of my face? No. A silly thought.

The portrait looks pretty good in my living room, but how I wish it could magically absorb my flaws so that I may be pretty forever.

My wish came true! The portrait bears the grimace of my malice. Must hide it in my attic. Fantastic! Who said that art was useless?

At the theater. The girl playing Juliet is the best I've ever seen. I think I shall seduce her. After all, I am so very pretty.

Funny: women are the bane of men's lives. Loving me has made her acting terrible. Art or life: choose! Except me, I can have both.

@Sibyl: It's over. I don't care who knows. Your acting is dreadful now, and I cannot live with a trivial woman. She killed herself. Typical!

People seem put off by my self-absorption. But I can't help but tell the truth about my excellence! It is important to be earnest, isn't it?

Sorry. I have been away. Got caught up in a sweet book about textiles. If I am so beautiful, my house should be as well!

Time goes on. I have become so decadent. Anyone ever tried opium? It's quite dreamy, especially when there are no consequences.

Basil refuses to speak to me. Even Lord Henry thinks I have become too corrupt. But how could I be corrupt with a face like this?

Decades and decades of terrible beauty! I live an everlasting and wonderful life, replete with lovers and objects of aesthetic quality.

Basil has seen the portrait. Being a true friend, I stabbed him in the front, and then blackmailed a queer chemist into burning the body.

Sibyl's brother tried to kill me. Tricked him. He was 'accidentally' shot. Dorian: a million; social mores: zero. Phil Spector: forget it.

It is too much! I must destroy the portrait. Now I prepare to age like a normal man . . .

Oops. Grew old all at once! Oh, the aesthete's life was a grand one, but one cannot escape morality and mortality in the end. Beauty is danger!

Of course, whosoever understands my tale will refrain from excess and flaunting social norms in their own life. Don't you think?

The Sorrows of
Young Werther
by Johann Wolfgang von Goethe

@SourKraut

Charming new town. I will finally be able to relax and be free of my troubles.

Met a new girl today! Need to avoid being trapped in the friend zone this time.

Lotte is my soulmate. Spent all day gazing at her. We even exchanged words. Nothing could persuade me that we are not meant to be together.

She is engaged to some dweeb named Albert. What kind of a name is Al?

This engagement has made me so sad. I thought our love would be pure! I sulk, I sulk. Woe is me.

Truly, I am so sad. I am overcome with despair. I feel nothing but sorrow.

Have I noted how upset I am? I am very upset. #pain #angst #suffering #sexdep

Must skip town for a bit and visit a friend. Create a plan to break off her engagement. She'll still be here when I get back.

Horrible! Horrible! Made a fool of myself before the whole aristocracy. Nothing in my life goes well! If only it could end.

Ach! I leave town for TWO DAYS and Lotte gets MARRIED? Does this mean my chances just got worse?

Much worse. No bookie would touch it. Woe is me. Consumed by a great sadness that I wonder if I've made clear enough yet.

D Lotte: Can I still visit you every day? If not I don't know WHAT I MIGHT DO. Not to scare you or anything.

My tears drown the whole Earth. This iPhone is drenched. How can a man in love restrain himself? Passion demands a dry outlet!

Though it pains me, I have become good friends with Lotte and Albert. Anything to stay close to her . . . so very close to her . . .

So I'm a bit of a whack job. Good thing no one's heard of restraining orders – or stalking – in all of Prussia. Otherwise out of luck.

D Albert: Hey bro. I'm going on a Journey. Mind sending along some pistols? Thanks.

One of us three must die. I have the pistols. A bullet for Albert, my rival? Or Lotte, my love? Or . . . me?

I am so very sad, far too sad to kill another human being. It must be me.

Lotte will feel bad after I shoot myself in the head and lie under a tree for twelve hours. She will run into my arms. Here goes!!

@WholeLotteLove
Werther's funeral today. Anyone going? I can't make it so somebody give my condolences and regards. Whatever. Thx.

The Sound and the Fury
by William Faulkner

@Mau'Benjamin

Golf. I love golf – that and my good sister. She smells like trees. Sure is cold out here! Hard to tweet, blind, with hands in my pockets.

There I go a' bellowin' again. Everyone tells me to hush but I think I am the only one who sees the terrible tragedy befalling my family.

I'm so disinclined to change. Apt metaphor for a Southern clan trying to resist the inevitable changes in the American Sou— ooohhh, a fire!

@Compson-OG
Though I escaped the South where my dying family drove me mad, Harvard remains a terrible and dreary place.

Also, why won't that watch stop ticking? Who needs watches? Doesn't everyone just count time in their head constantly like me?

Can't help believing I'll never truly escape my roots. My father's voice in my head. Reductio ad absurdum my fucking ass.

The image of other men's dicks in my sister also plagues me. So many dicks in my dear, dear sister.

Did I set her straight when the young man who knocked her up beat me up? If I could restore her virginity by will alone. Oh. Time for class.

Told father that we had committed incest. He refuses to believe me. At least I tell a tale better than my idiot brother Benjy.

Madness comes anyway as my mind rambles through thoughts of all the dicks in my dear sister. Also my own terror and neurosis.

The eye. The terrible eye. To Maine I go to escape Cambridge, and the dicks. The dicks. I must protect the women!

I keep forgetting to go to class. Impossible to focus on geometry with my sister's innocence angling through my head.

I can't express myself. I'm worse than Benjy in some ways. Perhaps that's irony. Don't know. Didn't go to class.

Mind fogged. Can think only about the tragedy of the Southern family. We are all mad in our own way. Where are those flat irons?

@Jas-Z

I'm surrounded by fools whose lives signify nothing. Dead father, suicidal brother, whore sister. My mother loves me and only me.

Time to get those Negroes working. It seems their family is on the rise, as ours moves ever closer to the grave.

@Dilsdo

Easter Sunday. Maybe finally find peace with these old crazy people. Taking Benjy with me to Church.

Oh God, this shit will never end. Crying and crying and the sound and the fury!

Everything has settled. We'll just go out for a nice Sunday ride in the carriage. Fuck. Took a wrong turn. Wailing and wailing. Epic fail.

The Story of My Life
by Helen Keller

@∷ ⠿⠿⠿⠿⠿ ⠿⠿⠿⠿⠿

The great tragedy of my life was when my dog jumped off a cliff because he had a ridiculous name.

Of this I was unaware, for I could not hear. The whole world sounded absurd, if you consider abysmal silence and eternal void absurd.

I constantly misbehaved, and disobeyed my parents. Little did they know I could not hear them. They mistook deafness for impertinence.

They wrote me notes. They yelled at me. They brought down right and proper discipline, but it was all a loss!

The truth dawned on them: I was both deaf and blind.

What a perfect storm of inconveniences. It's like a comedy of errors!

They punished me by rearranging the furniture, putting plungers in the toilet, and placing doorknobs on the walls.

I sustained a serious accident when I was ten, when I picked up the waffle iron. I burned my face even worse when they called back.

WHO IS THIS WOMAN WHO KEEPS PUTTING MY HANDS IN MY MOUTH. A PEDERAST? CAN SHE NOT HEAR ME SCREAM? I CAN'T.

- -

Of course I can't drive: not because I'm deaf, or blind, but because I'm a woman.

- -

People often confuse me with Anne Frank.

- -

This led to the best 'Overcoming Adversity' essay. The result: a blind, deaf, illiterate woman got into Harvard. And so did I.

- -

I believe the admissions officer thought I was ethnically diverse. You know: black. Or a foreigner. And a woman.

- -

Won't someone please at least pity–fuck me? Sex with a blind and deaf chick must at least be a novelty.

- -

Just don't put your hands in my mouth. I don't do that.

- -

I'm a really good premise for a joke. I mean, I'm literally disabled in every single way. It's kind of cheap comedy.

- -

I hope my physical disabilities won't overshadow my accomplishments.

- -

All Quiet on the Western Front
by Erich Maria Remarque

@RemarquableTale

I've always heard, 'Paul. Listen to adults, and teachers.'
You too? Well, don't. We could be in Hamburg cracking
open a Holsten instead.

Basic training was pretty soul-crushing. Corporal
Himmelstoss was a cruel martinet! Like the principal, but
school sucked more.

Life's been pretty rough here. The days pass, people die.
Soldiers don't get workman's comp, either.

Oh, we're just hanging out, waiting for bombs, snipers,
gas. Hate the poison gas most. That stuff really stings.

Corporal Himmelstoss showed up. What a fruit. He wants
to be our friend. Well fuck him, and his crazy German
last name.

It's summer. They say we're due a vacation . . . TO THE
FRENCH FRONT! This is gonna be a trip to remember.
Where's my camera?

We're just fighting, kickin' ass, not even taking names. Eat
my bayonet, clowns!

Summer vacation is over. Wow, a whole bunch of our
comrades died, didn't they? At least I have their pictures.

We are close to a town. We can finally get some poon–tank.

- -

The men I fight with are my brothers. We few, we happy few, we band of brothers. Oh, another one of my brothers got shot.

- -

I'm on patrol, and I see this French soldier. I beat him up. Then I look at his body and see that he's human, like me. *Quelle surprise!*

- -

I guess war is war.

- -

The war is going poorly for us Deutsche–folk. Never thought we'd lose. At least this will be the war to end all wars.

- -

I get to go home because of poison gas. I hope I don't die before we see the end of this –

- -

To Kill a Mockingbird
by Harper Lee

@BooScout

Thanks to Andrew Jackson, a series of commotions occurred resulting in my brother's arm being broken, dashing his hopes of gridiron glory.

More specifically, it all started when this wise-ass convinced us we should draw the town freak out of his basement.

Jem and Dill and I keep leaving him gifts, but he won't come out. But we're so young and innocent.

My brother has to babysit a morphine addict. She's ninety. It seems sketchy to me, but Dad says we just have to do it.

Why does Dad say such LAME shit? I don't want to walk a mile in ANYONE else's shoes. Toe jam, nail fungus, athlete's foot anybody? Gosh.

Dad always preaches about the 'right thing' and stuff. What does a heroic, moral single father/populist lawyer know about the right thing?

If I didn't know better, I'd say he was fighting for the REDS. Dirty pinko bastard.

My dad has been appointed to defend Tom Robinson. More like Uncle Tom Robinson, if you ask me.

Tom accused of raping a woman, but I'm pretty sure they just got it on. Can't a brother get some tush?

Went to the trial. Tom seems innocent. Also, it occurs that our town is full of racists. Perhaps only the eyes of a child can see the truth.

Is it weird that the youngest, least worldly-wise person in town comprehends reality most clearly? It's an insightful irony.

Dad totally embarrassed Boozer Bob. I'm sure this won't come back to bite us in some way. Also sure sun rises in the west.

A woman's house burned down. It was pretty sad watching her entire life go up in smoke and flames, except that fire is so AWESOME.

All-white jury convicted Tom. That was surprising. I figured ten minutes of deliberation meant that the verdict was close.

Dad out all night at the jailhouse. I don't really have a comment. He's a pretty cool guy. Good looking too, like Gregory Peck.

Please wear green in solidarity with Tom Robinson. He's totally, like, our Neda.

Uh oh. I think my innocence is gone. Also, Boozer Bob stalking us everywhere. It's getting kind of creepy.

On the way home. Hard to move fast in giant, silly costume. Is that Boozer Bob behind us again?

Long story short: Boozer Bob stalked us, tried to stab us, but Boo Radley FINALLY left the basement. Not sure what happened, but we're OK.

Boo Radley makes men fall on their own swords. He's like Octavian Caesar, and Boozer Bob is like Cassius with a brewski and gout.

The Life and Opinions of Tristram Shandy, Gentleman
by Laurence Sterne

@ACockAndBallsStory

Most narratives open as the story begins. I shall start at the night of my conception. Ever think about your parents doing *it*?

I'm not born yet, but I should begin my tale because I've got a long way to go and I tend to get distracted. Brace yourselves.

Still not born yet, but my parents are looking for a midwife, and boy, this midwife, she's got a whole life story, wanna hear?

AUTHOR'S PREFACE: Dear Sirs, you will find that my story is of great consequence, and a marvelous one indeed!

I've just been born, and I had a tragic accident. A windowpane fell on me, and flattened my dic— NOSE. My nose! That was almost embarrassing.

Chapter XIX: I don't feel like tweeting today.

Penso che sia migliore di non scrivere in inglese.

What a marvelous thing ******** today it was so *******
and indeed.

~!@#$%^(*&^%$##$%^&*(*&^%$#®√¨ø©®œˆ¨åƒ˙√¬˚©∂ß

Fantastic, no?? Aren't you glad you can follow my story and everything I say so effortlessly?

Alas poor Yorick, he dies, alone, in a dark room, much like any without lights, crying, as any widower, who's lost his wife.

Today I visited a marvelous young woman, tender, graceful, as any girl might be, which is her nature, much as absurdity is mine.

Today I was running around my chamber, yelling, animals fighting and killing, bleeding, caca and noise everywhere.

It was like an extended real-time version of the aristocrats without the incest.

My mother just entered and shouted 'WTF Tristram, again? What is all this nonsense?'

@Mom: It's a cock, piss, and shit story, Ma, and the fuckin' best of its kind, mother, the best of its motherfucking kind.

Tristram out, cya in the twentieth century, bitches.

Respectfully signed, ydnahS martsirT

Ulysses
by James Joyce

@StevieBlunder

Stately drunk Buck Mulligan came down the stairs singing about coronation day.

Milkman here. Good for those who don't have milk, who know not of milk. Tastes like the first milk I ever had, mother's sweet, warm milk.

What a dull day. Taught, walked, mused, contemplated God, composed a sonnet, and pissed on a rock in the park. What a day.

@DublinStateOfMind

Oh how hard it is to be a Jew. My daughter, who's a fine daughter, cannot be my son. Oh that I had a son.

I spotted a girl, and when I met her, whipped out my love rocket, lit the fuse, and let sparks fly from the end until it exploded.

Stephen and Buck are drinking in a hospital. Only in Dublin would a maternity hospital have a bar. Oh, those Irish.

Whan that quente hath birthed her childe into childhede it cryde, and here the scene shall I discryve.

When the child was born in Dublin, behold, came several drunk men from the town. For thou Dublin, in the land of Ireland, embraces him.

Now this child, mother born, as are we all, rather infelicitously for she is the most unwise of all god's creatures, was put into the world.

Leak on! Thou dark and wet placenta, leak on! Ten thousand men have fallen slithered out of thee in pain!

The baby began to speak. By now he was quite old and matured at a ripe age and the story of his life stopped making sense.

Yo son, that shit was intense. That baby was dumb-smart.

With my wife now, sitting in a field. I can't believe I jerked off in front of that girl. Oh well, what Molly don't know don't hurt.

My wife wants to mingle our love juices. AND she wants to have a whole conversation during? What's wrong with her?

I was a flower of the mountain, so we are flowers all a woman's body yes that was one true thing he said – Aw fuck it, u see where I'm going.

Whose idea was it to limit tweets to 140 characters, anyway? We really do live in a time of brevity.

Note from editor: Sorry, Jimmy, this means the story's gotta be drastically reduced in size. Make it punchy!

ORGASM

Venus in Furs
by Leopold von Sacher-Masoch

@SacherMasochist

Here's what turns me on: assertive, forward women who aren't afraid to say, hey baby, you're my personal property, get in that box.

What does Wanda mean when she says she doesn't understand how a golden shower can get me hot? Who isn't turned on by pee in the face?

Wanda has learned to love the master-slave dynamic. But she thinks me a fool for letting her dominate. I'm having a blast! She's the fool!

Being treated like a slave produces a super-orgasm. Like Superman's orgasm.

As the domination increases, the limit of sensuality approaches infinity. Math joke. Eat that, Leibniz.

Wanda wants to go to Florence.

Is it weird if I change my name to Gregor and act like her servant?

We're creating a domination scenario that doesn't exist. Pretending is part of the fun, because it's not real. Yes, mistress.

What should I call this fantastic game. Sex charades? ROLEPLAY! Score!

She hired a bunch of black chicks to abuse me. Are they doing me for the money or because of colonials' rage?

Wanda came home sad today. I asked if she wanted to talk. She took a dump on me. After all this time we still communicate. Amazing.

Wanda digs some new guy. I don't like the sound of this. She says she wants to 'submit' to HIM. Submit? She's one sick bitch.

The thought of Wanda engaging in perverse activity is a total bone-kill. I really don't want to play sex-charades today.

This new man is threatening and humiliating. I no longer desire to be her slave. What doesn't she understand about pets before bro's?

I'm so pissed. All I want to do is dominate women. That's what men do, we get on top and say: 'Baby, the ride's over when I'm over.'

I realize now that women should submit, and make me a sandwich while you're down there.

Men will always be on top, until women are our intellectual equals. Like that'll ever happen.

Waiting for Godot
by Samuel Beckett

@ShaggyGodotJoke

Sure have been waiting for a while. Gonna take my boot off and relax a bit. But I know a change's gonna come.

Boot won't come off. Frustrating, as is all of life. But nothing can be done, can it? Could be worse: boot up my ass.

Hanging from a tree to get a hard-on might help pass the time. Yeah, hard-ons are fun. And hard. And fun.

Ever heard the one about the brothel? There's this hooker, and she walks into a bar, and – oh, hold on, gotta take a piss.

What time is it, anyway? Is this ass-wind coming or not? Is this where I was supposed to meet him?

Wasn't even supposed to be here today, so sorry for the boring updates. Should have exciting news once Godot arrives.

Eating a carrot. Delicious carrot, but as I finish I realize that the malaise has not ended and the purposelessness of existence carries on.

I see some guy coming down the road. He told me his name: Pozzo. Almost as retarded as my name, Estragon. WTF?

I can't understand what this crazy asshole is talking about. And he just said cunt.

Pozzo reminds me of the gimp from *Pulp Fiction*? Boy, that scene was fucked up.

Where is this asshole? @Vlady: Are you sure it's tonight? I'm telling you, he isn't coming! Just fell in a ditch. That sucked.

Still waiting. A boy told us that Godot was going to be late. OH REALLY?

So there's a dog and the dog has fleas, you know what fleas are? A thing on a dog, this dog, and the dog has fleas, you know what dogs are . . .

Jeez. Our lives are so boring.

Pozzo is back. He is blind now, which has gained him much inSIGHT. Wordplay!

Godot not here/coming yet again. Contemplated suicide but the rope was too short. Perhaps tomorrow.

Still waiting. Trying not to think of this awful, frustrating situational metaphor we've found ourselves stuck in.

Shit, I just lost the Game.

Watchmen
by Alan Moore

@Rorschizzle

A comedian died tonight. He was all about the lulz. No one laughed.

I should warn the Nite Owl, but first I should break into his house and eat all his beans. Classy.

It turns out not everyone is as paranoid as I am; they don't think that they - you know, THEY - are out to get us.

Funeral was melancholy. It's perfect and moving in the rain. Can you request the rain metaphor as part of the pre-need package?

Must break into a military facility and visit Doctor Manhattan. I hate seeing him, he's always waving his big blue dong around.

I fuckin' knew it! It's like he's all-knowing but lacks the knowledge and the etiquette of putting your junk away when guests arrive.

Doctor Manhattan is cancerous, and someone tried to shoot Ozymandias. What a fruitcake.

Some turdblossom framed me, and now I'm going to be arrested. Maybe I can take out some cops for fun.

In jail, but still managed to totally burn one cop with a flame-thrower. He was on freakin' fire. (No fucks in comics.) It was pretty bomb.

Hey: I'm not stuck in this rathole with you. You're stuck with me. Did you catch what I did to that guy with all the burning oil?

There's a big prison riot. I want my face back; what's a man without his face? A faceless man, that's what. Can't face that.

Laurie and Nite Owl came to get me. They're all flushed and red. I think they got it on. Super-awkward. Now I have to ride with them.

Yeah, they definitely balled. Hold on, I have to crush a midget into a toilet. Pwnd.

Ozymandias was behind the attacks. I knew it, you can never trust a fruitcake who dances with Warhol at Studio 54.

Nite Owl says we have to go to Antarctica. Frostbite on your nads can seriously lower your sperm count.

We have to fight Ozymandias. He's like the two of us combined, on crack, no, steroids. No, speed. We're screwed.

Manhattan appeared and kicked ass. Deus ex manhactica. The ass-kicking was even more impressive with that huge blue dong waving everywhere.

Now 'they' are gonna unleash giant squids in the world's major cities! Either I stop this or I stop drinking the water.

Everyone disagrees? You express your complex conception of morality, I explain mine, then you blow me into little sociopathic pieces?

Fuck. Oops.

Mrs Dalloway
by Virginia Woolf

@FlowerGirl

Ah! A party tonight! Should be a fine time – fun, friends, nothing stressful, nothing awkward. Should be a blast!

And I've got these lovely, lovely flowers. Need only now to prepare my house for this fine even— oh my God it's Peter.

He thinks I don't love my husband because of him. The secret is, I don't love my husband because I dig chicks.

On a side note, has anybody noticed that @Septimus's posts have become a little erratic since the war ended?

Really, he used to love Shakespeare and poetry. Now he's like the Bard of SADford upon Lame-on.

It's alright though, he's probably suffering from a lack of proportions. I mean, sure most of his friends died but think how many lived??

Ah, my husband is home! He's brought me a bundle of roses! I bet he loves m— well, this is just uncomfortable.

A void exists between my husband and me. It's as if I am . . . different, somehow. I'm not sure what one would call it, though.

Now this awful woman has come to teach my daughter. Ah, how I hate this bitch. Really, everyone in my life is stressing me out today . . .

So, Septimus's doctors decided he really was insane. Taking their advice, he decided to take the plunge . . . out a tenth-story window.

- -

Finally, time for the party! Though I'm not sure how I'm feeling about it now, to be honest. All these assholes kind of make my life hell.

- -

I identify with Septimus though, more than these awful people who make Victorian life so open to criticism . . .

- -

Because, I'm not sure if you realize, but Victorian life is backwards. Really backwards. These people are insane.

- -

Perhaps I should jump out of a window too, that might get me away from this ridiculous, oppressive society.

- -

Or a river. Yeah, that's it. A river.

- -

Crime and Punishment
by Fyodor Dostoevsky

@RobPeterPayPaul

It's hard being a poor student – lots of work, crappy room, and I have the ugliest hat this side of the Urals.

Man at the bar telling me a story. In essence: 'Now my daughter's a prostitute, and I know why (yeah yeah) because I got high.' Or drunk.

Though I must say, his daughter is quite the lady. Very comforting, though a bit pushy with the Jesus stuff.

It is a bit of a rut being so miserably impoverished. I need something to lighten up my life, something exciting . . .

I've got it. Rather than accept financial aid from my friend, I'll murder an elderly moneylender in cold blood. Why? I'm not telling.

Really, I'm not telling. Probably something to do with that hack Turgenev and that hip nihilism shit, but my lips are sealed.

However, if you'd like to guess at my psychological and ideological motivations for the next couple of hundred years, be my guest.

Sorry about the rant there. Will try to keep the long, introspective monologues to a minimum.

Casually off'd that old maid while typing this. Some other bitch just walked in . . . well, she's dead too. Bad timing, LOL.

There's no evidence, I have no motive. The police think they're going to solve this one? I'm a Napoleon. I can do whatever I want.

Though you'd think since I just wrote a thesis on committing and getting away with crimes, there might be some cause for suspicion?

You know, maybe I don't have as much emotional fortitude as I thought I did. I'm starting to feel a bit guilty. Should pass.

I'M REALLY UPSET RIGHT NOW BECAUSE I KILLED AN OLD WOMAN AND THOUGH I TWEET IT MY LIPS CAN'T SPEAK IT.

I think the coppers are starting to get suspicious on account of my acting LIKE A CRAZY PERSON WHO KILLED AN OLD WOMAN.

If you could spare a few hours, I'll tell you about the intricate details of my very simple moral dilemma. Try to listen through my tears.

I wish I could just shout it on the streets, then I think no, because everyone would look at me weird. Because killing old women is weird.

I cracked and told @StSofia, which was a weird choice since the second lady I killed was her friend. She didn't seem too upset, though.

Perhaps Jesus could help with some of these guilt issues. Religion against my ideals though – same ideals that made me kill that woman.

Alienation too much. Confessed to my crime – being sent to Serbian prison. Only seven years though, and Sofia loves me for some reason?

Another day in the old jail cell. Everything seems pretty bleak. Other prisoners hate me, and there's nothing much to do.

Oh hey, it's the New Testament. I'd like to suggest that this book is going to change my life, but that's really a story for another time . . .

Wuthering Heights
by Emily Brontë

@HeathBar

A family has found me, and they keep calling me gypsy.
Have I stolen their wallets yet? NO.

They're all miserable excuses for people. They hit me and
treat me like I'm bonkers. Or a gypsy. Except Catherine,
she's pretty cool.

The maid is also very nice, but she's a maid, you know?
They're like slaves. I guess I am a gypsy, so not much
better.

Catherine very clearly likes me, and I like her too. I hope
we can spend the rest of our lives together.

Get off of her you motherfucking dogs, fucking devils.

Apparently is not OK for little kids to swear that way.
Catherine now stays with another family, and I'm not
allowed to see her.

I want to see her. She wants to see me. Can't we be
together? Catherine's brother is a total ass. Sorry. A pence
for the cursing jar.

Enough. This home is miserable. Everyone is cruel. I'm
leaving. They'll be sorry.

After a time I've become rich and successful, and very
good-looking. This ought to mess with their heads
back home.

I can't believe it. Catherine has married the twatting tool across the street.

The house is now mine. Since the neighbor has Catherine, I'll seduce his sister. We'll see how brave he is when she's got Heathcock in her.

Girl is preggers. Catherine is dead. My world is over. I've become an evil, evil man. Naming my son Heathcliff Jr.

ALL I WANT TO DO IS BEAT MY WIFE. RAGE!!! PASSION! HEAT!!! HEATH!!

Jr's been bad. He must stay locked in his room without food. Wiseass. I should have pushed his mother down a flight of stairs earlier!!

I'm dying. Life has been meaningless. Oh Catherine!

My dying wish: that my spirit be united with Catherine's, that we roam the heath together forever, and that Kate Bush writes a song about us.

Lolita
by Vladimir Nabokov

@PolanskiFan106

- -

OK guys, yes, my name is Humbert Humbert. Let's try to be mature about this.

- -

I need to find a place to stay where I can write. My work is important. No pets, no noise, no distractions of ANY sort!!

- -

Did I just see a Nymphet – or was it my fertile writer's imagination? They're like sex goddesses, but mini. So like, SkineMax at Gymboree.

- -

This girl is a goddess. I must rent this room. Then I'll get her to come over, put on some music, crack the vino. And make some magic.

- -

Her name is Lolita. But her mother, Charlotte, is obsessed with me. I should bail but damn, her little honey of a daughter is FINE.

- -

When I was twelve, I was hot for twelve-year-olds. What's changed? Nothing, as far as I can tell. I am in a haze, or soon hope to be.

- -

@Charlotte: I have a diary on my desk, please don't look at it. It's personal, also incriminating. Tempted yet?

- -

Problem suddenly solved. Lolita's mom got hit by a car. Thank goodness, now I can get down to business.

- -

@Lolita: Time to come home from camp. Your mom is, uh, sick?

- -

Ohhh, this hotel looks classy. Enchanted Hunters, sounds mythical. More like Enchanted Humpers, n'est-ce pas?

@Lolita: Do you smoke after sex? Oh wait, you're too young to smoke. But still, would you like a smoke . . . after?

There's a guy who looks just like me. He's kind of cool but follows us in his car. Yet with a name like Clare Quilty . . . What, me worry?

Lolita must have an education. She can't be simply an ignorant whore. I like a girl with brains. Looks aren't everything after they turn thirteen.

I got a flyer for a school play. It's called *The Enchanted Hunters*. Quilty again!

Lolita is sick. We must get her out of this school. It's Clare Creepy. I'm the good guy this time, for a change!

No! Little Lo-lo has disappeared from the hospital. I am her immediate kin. Who authorized this?

I'm gonna find that Quilty fucker and stab him in the face. That's what he deserves for stealing my almost-a-woman!

Later. Found him but Lolita was not with him. She got away. He wanted to make a porno with her, that sick fuck. She's just a kid!

So you see, ladies and gentlemen of the jury, I'm not so bad after all. No, I'm a good person. Please let me off?

Can you imagine me in jail? Not for pedophilia, but for murder. You're never in for what you deserve. Sigh. So let me tell you a story.

Gulliver's Travels
by Jonathan Swift

@LittleBigMan

Though I have made a life as a surgeon, I do enjoy a good travel. In this day and age, 'tis not hard at all to acquire a ship and crew.

All goes well thus far upon the sea. My men are loyal, and I do believe I captain this vessel well. Oh shit! A ROCK!

Awoke in an unfamiliar land. The boat and my crew are gone. Oh dear, the people here are very small. Oops. Sorry about that.

I don't mean to boast; I'm not a terribly tall man. But these people of Lilliput are the size of child's Johnson. Still, they have captured me.

I have become a great favorite of the Lilliputian court, whose antics are like an adorable tiny version of King George's, the blithering idiot.

These tiny men are very serious, and engaged in a war with their neighbors. Plus they don't like me calling them 'shorty' and 'junior'.

Helped them by stealing the enemy fleet, as if playing like a boy in the bathtub. But they demand 'Blefuscudian delendum est' and I say no.

The Lilli-fuckers have decided to blind me. Luckily, I am twelve times their size and escape was not difficult. Back to England!

I feel compelled to set out again. This time I shall have to improve my captaining.

Again my crew has abandoned me. Oh dear! Woke up to see a gentleman over seventy feet tall. What a clever turn of events! Now I'M dick-sized.

I have been turned into something of a traveling novelty. I even have a little house. All goes well. OH SHIT, AN EAGLE.

Home in England. Yet I am compelled to set out again. Wife seems skeptical; what does she know? Hope things go well this time.

Attacked by pirates who left me marooned on an island. Starting to understand why I'm the 'captain of several ships'. Don't tell my wife.

Picked up by flying city. They've invented bombs and the computer. In the seventeenth century. Perhaps I'll see the foresight of this in 300 years.

Back in England. Never traveling again. Ever. OK, maybe one more time. Just one more time.

Marooned again. How many ships have I lost now? Oh well. There Is an extremely ugly, stupid man here. He can't speak or reason, it seems.

This island is run by horses. Beautiful, wonderful, brilliant horses. They are perfect beings. The man I saw earlier is their slave.

Horses amused by my spark of intelligence. Yet, my ability to lie is a 'threat' to their society and I must be expelled. Can't I stay, please?

Back home. I cannot stand human society. I have taken to wearing horse shit about my neck as my wife's smell repulses me.

In the stable, brushing my horse. I should be here most of the day, and for the rest of my life.

The Wall
by Jean-Paul Sartre

@SpanishToms

God this room is bright. How much did I have to drink last night? Oh right, nothing but the stinging nectar of my own angst.

Guards wanted to know where Ramón Gris is. Didn't tell them anything. I'm not a rat, though rat sounds good right now. I'm awfully hungry.

In a cell. Not so bad, except one kid seems very nervous. Another guy talks about how in Morocco they trample prisoners to save ammo.

@GreyJuan: I don't think they'll run us over here. Don't worry. They won't run us over. Unless, you know, they're really low on ammo.

Sentenced to death. Never really thought of death before. No reason. Have reason now, on account of my being executed in the morning.

I feel pity for the kid, but his inability to cope with his completely cruel and arbitrary execution without tears bugs me for some reason.

A doctor is here. Normally I would talk, but I didn't feel like it. The trivialities of life have begun to fall away.

The kid is trembling and asking if it hurts to be killed by a firing squad. His fear of pain and suffering bother me more than my execution.

As the night goes on, I've started to think maybe it isn't so bad to be a bit upset by this whole ordeal.

Picturing the execution in my head over and over, like a song I can't stop humming to myself – except it ends with 4,000 holes in ME.

In a way, I'm already dead. The doctor is fascinating as a man who, by virtue of not being about to be dead, is truly alive.

Still, in a way, his impending death is just like ours – just less clear. I suppose life is pretty bleak, huh? Can't even LOL.

If I'd known I'd be shot like this, I wouldn't have spent a moment chasing girls or talking at anarchist meetings.

But if I'd known, and then not gone to meetings, I wouldn't be here. So I wouldn't know. Then I'd go to meetings. This is heavy, man.

I want to die cleanly. I'm not sure why, tho. In theory, death's meaninglessness should invalidate any dignity taken from life, right?

The big morning's here. They'll take me out to that wall, that terrible, terrible symbol of the absolute nature of inevitable death.

They keep asking me where Ramón Gris is and promise to let me go if I tell them. But I am a true revolutionary. I face death with dignity.

It would be pretty hilarious though if I just told them some nonsense and sent their soldiers on a wild goose chase, huh?

@TheSoldiers: Ramón Gris? He's in the graveyard. He's hanging out with the dead, just like me. Parallelism is vital to deathbed humor.

True humor: Ramón Gris actually IS in the graveyard. And now he's going to be killed. And so I'm free. I LOL'd so hard I cried.

Pride and Prejudice
by Jane Austen

@FirstThoughtBestThought

Usually a man wills his home to his wife or kids. But sometimes, he wills it to a distant relative, so when he dies, you're out on your ass.

And then, and THEN, that distant, meddlesome priest of a relative tries to seduce one of your sisters.

Unsure why anyone would want my sisters. All they want is to hit it with the officers – what war are they even fighting in the countryside?

Though my older sister – Jane – is nice. How could she not be? Jane is such a good name. I would like anybody named Jane.

The English country is a dull place much of the time. Local dances, hysterical family, long, long afternoons with nothing much to do . . .

Oh shit, some rich young gentlemen just showed up. Score!

This one man seems quite interested in my sister – but the other, a Mr Darcy, is very cold and condescending. I find that . . . attractive.

It's as if the less he seems to care about me, the more drawn to him I am. This seems like the opposite of how it should be? Oh well.

But I do hear bad things about this Mr Darcy and they have begun to repulse me. Nothing ruins infatuation for a lady like hearsay.

That other dude dumped my sister, and him and Darcy left town. What a mean, mean man! He's terrible! Oh, he wants to marry me.

Really let Darcy have it – over my sister, and that officer he cheated. Said I'd never marry such a bad man. Never. Absolutely never.

Isn't it cool how I'm defying my gender role by standing up for myself? My whole family, though flawed, does make a strong claim for women.

Just received a letter from Darcy. Taking a look.

Huh. I guess he wasn't such a bad guy. Maybe everything had an explanation. Maybe I do like him, just a little bit . . . best not think of it.

Sorry, it's been a few months. Out in Darcy's land now – touring his estate. Quite nervous to see him . . .

So Darcy is here. He's handsome, charming – everything. We're ABOUT to make the magic happen when my STUPID sister disappears with some guy!

Hunt continues for @Lydia – has she tweeted any clues as to her whereabouts? Check @Wickham too – he's the deadbeat.

So @Lydia and @Wickham actually married in secret. Well, as long as they're married, their disappearance and sexual escapade is OK, I think.

Meanwhile, Jane – wonderful, sweet Jane – is also married. We're dropping like flies! I suppose I love Darcy now, after all of this.

He and I are wed and have moved to our own home in the country. I got the man, his money, and uh . . . women's power!

Sir Gawain and the Green Knight

@GawainsWorld

Cruel fate has landed me on King Arthur's b-squad. Lancelot frogged his damsel and we all know it, but he's top dog. WTF?

So listen here, some green man came to the hall and wants someone to cut his head off. Some sort of dare? Could be fun, right?

The deal is I cut off his head now, and he cuts off mine a year later. What a jester – doesn't he know he'll be dead?

This goblin fellow is totally dead.

All seemed fine until Ichabod Crane here fell to the floor, stood up, and picked up his head. His head, in his hands. In HIS HANDS!

Oh boy, I've really soiled the kettle now. I gotta skip out of Camelot, honor my word, and find this devil so he can reciprocate.

I had it coming. 'Yeah Gawain, come over, we'll have a good time, open some champagne, have some ham, it'll be fun.' Arthur, you prick.

This is the last time I get drunk with the Sirz. It's never happening again because I'LL BE DEAD!

I'm bumping my nads on this horse, looking for someone who will kill me. He cannot be killed. Also, it's Nativity festival season.

I found this castle in the woods. The lady here wants to pull Excalibur from my stones, if you know what I mean.

The owner wants to make a deal. He says that whatever I earn there I have to give to him in exchange for what he earns? Why not.

Wait, wait, if I get on his woman, then logically, on my honor, I would have to sleep with him . . .

I'm not doing that. I almost did a man when we were trying to kill that dragon in Ireland and thought we had ten minutes to live. That was awkward.

His wife gave me a silk scarf which she SAYS will keep me from harm. Couldn't hurt, right. I'm basically fated anyway. Ugh, fate.

Forget the deal with her husband. I'm not giving him a scarf that could save me. If Mr Stevie Wonder believes in superstition, so can I.

Time to go meet my fate. I should have never cut off that guy's head. How did I not see this coming? Because it's completely unpredictable.

You think if you cut off someone's head, he'll die, but not in Camelot. Fucking Camelot. Maybe the scarf will help.

He's gonna cut off my head now! If only I had heeded Sir Rae Kwon's timeless advice – protect ya neck. Ugh, Faugh my lyfe.

He didn't do anything, he just nicked me. Turns out it was the woman's husband. We're leaving on peaceful terms.

Note to self: in the future, don't cut off anybody's head if they might come back and cut off mine. Could be a trap!

The Adventures of Huckleberry Finn
by Mark Twain

@declineofwesternsiv

Seems like soon as a fella comes into a bit o' money, everyone comes out of the woodworks after'n it.

These ladies wants to sivilize me? More like reverse gold-dig my fame and fortune. @FencinTom: Get me outta here!

Escaped the house, but my drunkard Pap showed up. I reckon he is all kinds of bad for my development, locking me up in his cabin and all.

I just want to be free and have adventures and whatnot. Also, keep Pap's hands off my damn money.

Faked my own death. Headin' down the Mississippi. Ran into the gold-digger's former slave, Jim, trying to escape to Illinois.

Not sure how I feel about this. Don't think a slave ought to escape, on account of his being vital property and all.

Found a house floating on the river. Jim found a body but wouldn't tell me who it was. Probably not a big deal.

You know, the more I talk to Jim, the more I get to thinkin', 'Boy, these Negroes is just like other people. Maybe they shouldn't be owned.'

Really though, what do you all think? I'm beginning to think that buyin' and sellin' peoples is immoral or something.

Tried out going in drag. Don't really want to talk about it. Long story short: being a lady is much more than a pretty dress.

I sure do live in a confounding hypocritical and silly world. This is why I ain't getting sivilized – cuz sivilization is crazier than me!

OH WTF! THEY SHOT MY ONLY FRIEND!! CAN'T TWEET, TOO UPSET. FUCK. FUCK. FUCK.

Picked up two guys. One says he's king of France, other an English duke. Weird. Why would royalty move to America to become scam artists?

On an unrelated note, I saw a man give a moving oration on the cowardice of a lynch mob. Had nothing to do with my adventure, but touching.

The goddamned king went and sold Jim! Some friend. I really thought I could trust the fellow, him being French and all.

In a pretty convenient twist of fate, it turns out Jim got sold to old Tom Sawyer's relations.

They think I'm Tom. Tom came – he says he's my brother. Tom has hatched an elaborate plan to free Jim.

Need to ponder slave morality one last time. I suppose, in the end, slavery is probably a bad idea, considering reparations and all.

Sprang Jim out. He's free, I'm free, all seems well.

Oh wait. Jim was already free by order of the law, and Tom knew it. He just wanted to have an adventure. LOL.

Frankenstein
by Mary Shelley

@NotoriousDOC

I often think of the craziest thing I could get away with using my MD.

Digging up body parts and putting them together seems pretty out there. Maybe add a million volts of electricity?

Just did a bit-torrent-style grave robbery. My new 'man' will be an artful collage. Also, good conversation starter.

It's alive! I'd better beat it over the head repeatedly with a fire extinguisher.

So sometimes you build something, and it gets away. They're gonna can me at the university if they find out about this.

Jeez, the monster is killing people. Wonder if this will be more professionally embarrassing than getting caught with a black hooker?

I've just received word that my brother has been killed. It's that lying bitch of a maid! Let's kill her!

Not the maid. It was the monster. He learned how to fool the whole CSI team by planting evidence. He's good. I guess I'm responsible?

This killing thing is getting way out of control. You know, like a mistress you can't shut up?

I'm definitely not responsible for this.

When I put the body together it was all for the HaHa. I didn't think it would live. And why must an abomination kill as its first instinct?

It's time to take a trip. Want to hear some really great, extended scenery descriptions? I'm an aspiring poet, so don't judge me.

D PromethianOG: Honestly dude, chill the fuck out bro. Stop killing shit. I'm getting fucked for it. Could lose my tenure.

Now I'm sick, and in jail. Are you happy?

Good, bail allowed. I had to use my card though. At least I'll get miles.

You know who's kind of hot? My cousin. I'm gonna marry her.

Not fair. The monster just killed my cousin/wife. This is over. Either one of us, or both must join her.

I followed the asshole's trail to the North Pole. Maybe Santa will have some eggnog for me.

The monster I chased for all these months just killed me, then killed himself. And for irony, he did it on my pyre. FML.

All the Pretty Horses
by Cormac McCarthy

@AllthingsbeingEquus

My grandfather is dead. My father is broken by the war. I am too young to take over the ranch. It will be sold.

The Texas I love is dying. The frontier lies only across the border – to Mexico.

Rawlins says he'll come with me. Our manly journey across the sparse landscapes of the south will serve as the stuff of American folklore.

Ran into some crazy kid. Perfect complement to my thoughtful stoicism! Riding a crazy horse, perhaps he will accompany us.

THUNDERSTORM!

Kid ran off, thinking he is destined to be hit by lightning. Has anybody seen a big white horse around?

Found horse. Kid stole it. Ran off. What now? Need a job.

Found jobs on a ranch. Good food, free room. Comely daughter.

<3 <3 <3 Horses <3 <3 <3

Long courtship. The daughter is drawn to my mythic character and insightful if rare words.

Her aunt went on some crazy duty and honor rant. Just let the girls be, beotch!

Arrested. Stuck in Mexican prison. Just like spring break, hah!

Everyone is my enemy. I think I've lost my youthful naiveté. World is hard.

Shank! Shank shank shank! Who knew stabbing someone got you out of jail?

Tried to win back the lady. She won't come with me! 'Duty' and 'honor'. Code for FRIGID, amiright?

Back in Texas. Nothing is resolved.

I remain confused by the simultaneous horror and wonder of the empty world. However, I am wiser for the experience.

Don't worry. I still love horses. I am the model of a man.

Or is liking horses this much kind of girlie? That would really cramp my point here.

Swann's Way
by Marcel Proust

@RaidersOfTheLostTime

- -

I can't wait for Mom to tuck me in. Perhaps I'm too old for this, but then I see light in the hall as she approaches and think, Nah!

- -

My father wants me to stop behaving like such a little momma's boy in front of the guests, but what does he know?

- -

Aunt is such a big part of life. She's also a big pain in the *derrière*. But ohhh, those snack-cakes make me so HOT.

- -

Summer is over. I'm sad about leaving the country house, but don't know why. The flowers here mean so much to me. BTW: Aunt dead.

- -

My neighbor Swann is quite a guy, I hear he used to be a real stud.

- -

@BotSwanna
I'm not too popular, except that the grandmas and the geriatrics really do love me.

- -

I saw a *fille* tonight at dinner. Total 10. She seems so sweet. And well-intentioned. And innocent.

- -

I took her home. She was wearing a symbolic vagina-flower, and I touched it gently, slowly, subtly, unnoticeably, and went to bed with her.

- -

Remember when I took that girl home? I do it every day. I'm nuts about this one. She's mine, and nobody else's.

- -

Turns out she's a *putain* hooking up with other girls and servicing men on yachts. I heard it through the grapevine.

Oh god, this is terrible, the worst thing that's ever happened. My life's finished, everyone hates me, even my lover. I want to die.

Never mind. She's not even my type. All that time wasted on a girl that I didn't even really dig.

@RaidersOfTheLostTime
What a story huh . . . *salopes* ain't *merde* but hos and tricks, huh? I'm glad childhood is free of women.

I met Swann's daughter on the street. It's funny how I'm getting a crush on her the way Swann did on that other girl.

My life feels bereft of purpose whenever I am away from her!

I'm an adult now, and that woman, well, Swann married her. No, not his daughter. Time seems so bizarre. It's always playing tricks on me.

. . . Toying with my perception of reality, not ever making sense, never quite belonging to me, nor to anyone else, but rather remaining a –

. . . Force of contiguous moments gently grazing upon one another for our own satisfaction and convenience.

Wow. Time flies when you're writing books.

The Aeneid
by Virgil

@TranslatioStud

Got a gift of a huge wooden horse today, here in Troy. Just appeared outside the city gate. BTW: War going poorly.

Surprise. Soldiers inside the horse. We didn't start the fire! Hector's Ghost says to GTFO – take Dad and the kid with me.

I'm on a boat. Three generations of Aenean men on a sea-journey of epic proportions. Hmm. Sounds familiar . . .

Stopped over in the Big C. Met a cool chick. She has issues with her previous marriage, but hey: people can change! Right?

In a cave with a super-freaky woman who – fondles livers! Oh, and she can tell the future!

Relationship moving too fast. Said I wanted to play the Elysian field but Carthage rings with weddings bells. More like death knells.

@Dido: Hey girl, yeah, you my world baby, yeah girl I love you, but I have a city to found and Juno says to get moving. Duty before hos.

In a nutshell: I told her I was leaving, so she lit a fire and went the way of the . . . Dido. #badbreakups

WAR! Why can't we be friends??

Going downriver into Hades on my boat. This whole journey really does feel awfully familiar. Can't place it.

@AugustusRex: Check out my descendants. As you can see, you're the most glorious, so glorious that you no doubt fund the poets of your time.

Juno being very difficult considering she charged me with this task. Why do women always do the opposite of what you tell them?

I must assemble an army with the king of Arcadia, and Elrond, Elf-king of Rivendell.

We're gonna take these Guineas out! My boy Pallas is on that.

We need reinforcements, our lines are falling apart.

Turnus wants a fight. Time to treat him Aaron Burr style.

Finally, we have peace. Rome is settled. The great fraternity of civilizations can begin. Pax Bromana.

The Devil in the Flesh
by Raymond Radiguet

@DevilInMyHeart

What can I say? Is it my fault that I like women? I am sure people will criticize me for this, but who cares?

The first sexual encounter I had was when I was little. I sexually harassed a girl with a letter I wrote. Boy, her mom was pissed.

I met a girl named Marthe. I will lend her books. The ladies dig it when you talk about books.

Turns out Marthe is married. My life is a dismal disaster. I just want to run home and cry!

I ran into Marthe on a boulevard today. Her husband is off at war. This is my opportunity!

Sometimes I wonder about the morality of sleeping with a soldier's wife. But it won't stop me from trying.

Marthe just wants to be friends. Why am I always in the friend-zone? Perhaps if I touch her inappropriately this will change.

Oh la vache! She's kissing me. Totally missed the signs.

I'm having an affair, and I'm only sixteen. I hope her husband isn't in Special Ops. He could easily mess me up if he found out. Oh, her too.

While leaving Marthe's home a kid saw me on the stairs. He grinned and betrayed me.

My parents found out about my affair. Mom was upset. She would rather I not home-wreck. Prude. My dad lol'd.

Wouldn't it be funny if I seduced Marthe's best friend. After all, Marthe's got a husband. It's only fair.

Her friend is a foreigner and doesn't know the language so well, including the word 'no'. We messed up Marthe's sheets.

Marthe found out. I convinced her that her friend and I were just hanging out . . . more like rockin' out. With my cock out.

Marthe is pregnant. I'm too young to be a baby-daddy. Why did I believe her about the pills that haven't been invented yet?

She wants to keep it. I told her I didn't. She left. I still love her. Her husband thinks it's his. Boy, is he in for a surprise.

Marthe and I must separate. I don't want to, but I suppose it's best. I did love her.

I haven't seen Marthe in months. My life feels empty.

Today my brother came home and told me that Marthe's brother was an uncle. I guess I am a father.

Marthe is dead. And few people know about our affair. I must keep on with my life as though nothing happened. At all. Ever. Kid? What kid?

You think that after all these years people would write new things. But no, we all just love reading about insolent, troublesome teenagers.

Dracula
by Bram Stoker

@BleedingGums

A former student of mine called. He wants me to do a house call.

A damsel is bleeding from her ears and eyes! She's afraid of the sun! Like a ginger!

We must sort this out. She may be a vampire, but I can't tell the father. He wonders if her 'lady times' are just out of control.

Sadly, the patient is dead. Reports have come in of an undead woman terrorizing the town's people. A connection? Maybe.

Her fiancé has returned. Funny, since there's all these suitors here, since, you know, we thought the fiancé was, you know.

Fiancé says his Transylvanian client turned out to be an undead, blood-sucking monster intent on coming to England. A connection? Possible.

This monster seems to have heard about our plot to kill him. He's smart. Guess 'monster' is not synonymous with retard.

D Mina: Hey, I think your new boyfriend is kind of a creep. Just take it slow, OK? I'm not sure about him.

Of course, she was seduced by Dracula. Some BDSM activity. It would be easier to deal with him if this whore could keep her knickers on.

We Sharpied her face and shaved her eyebrows, and now we're hypnotizing her. Doesn't seem to help a bit.

Somehow, this woman psychically knows where Dracula is. Everyone in the carriage! We're moving out!

The Dracu–GPS hypnosis gimmick is starting to fail. I guess this very stylistic inconvenience will force us to explore new options.

We have reached Transylvania just before sunset. Dracula is being transported here by gypsies – of course.

Caught up, but they GYPED old Quincey. Luckily, we managed to kill Dracula.

Really, it wasn't that hard.

OK, OK. All we did was jam a knife into his heart. Why, after 1,000 years, could nobody figure that out?

No. Not a wooden knife. A knife knife. Forget the garlic and the cross. Whatever.

Why the knife? He touches the soul and body. Only his heart is vulnerable. Shit. I just killed the greatest Romantic hero ever, didn't I?

The Rime of the Ancient Mariner
by Samuel Taylor Coleridge

@RamblinMan

On my way to a wedding. A bum approaches. What does he want? Sorry. I don't have any money, bro. Go busk for change elsewhere.

He needs to tell me a story. Yes, I know: you lost your house in a fire, you did drugs, your daughter needs clothes, you're a veteran.

Hey, stop staring at me like that. OK, OK. I'll listen. Make it quick.

@MaritimeMan

On a ship with sailors, we were doing pretty well. We know what's up and what's down. We know that we were sailing south.

But then a storm. A perfect storm. The Weather Channel said it would be sunny. Assholes!

Can you guess where we ended up? Yeah, the worst place ever. Antarctica. So, so cold. We should have shopped at North Face first.

How cold? Have you been to Chicago? Imagine that, but 100x worse. And with only an all-male crew, don't ask how we stay warm at sea.

Then t'was a huge bird overhead. Let me tell you, enormous. The biggest I've ever seen. Perhaps a sign from God. Or an albatross.

We figured, well, we're pretty screwed, so why not follow this bird? If nothing good comes of it, at least it'll be something to do.

I, too, needed things to do. I looked up and thought, That's a pretty cool bird. I want that bird. So I shot it with my crossbow.

Boy oh boy, was the crew pissed. My arrow slew their good fortune as it did the bird! Who knew?

When our fate improved, they weren't pissed. When it got worse, they were pissed. Moody scurvy scum. Take a pill.

We were stuck in some silent and becalmed waters. Acqua acqua everywhere, but non si puo bere. Maybe I shouldn't have shot the bird.

As punishment I was made to wear the bird around my neck. 'Twas a cool symbolic thing. A burden. I'd ROFL but for my arthritis.

Soon we encountered a ghost-ship. Like in that movie, *Pirates of the Caribbean*, or *Return of the King*, I can't remember which.

The crew played craps for our souls, and of 200 mates only I survived.

So here I am, wandering the earth, stopping strangers on the street, chatting them up with my tale.

- -

And if I don't, a pain in my heart comes, a pain that a Tums can't even touch.

- -

So anyway, have a good time at the wedding.

- -

The Waste Land
by T. S. Eliot

@DeadFlowers

Note from Ezra Pound: Maybe cut 75%?

Let us go then, Marie and I, when winter's warmth is spread throughout the sky like a dead lilac breeding out in April.

I remember when I was young we'd tread down the cobbled winterpath to the Biergarten, and drink us a few brewskis.

When we were entirely too smashed to keep on drinking, the barkeep would say: *Hurry up, please, it's time.*

I would stand over the urinal, drunk, full of fluid, screaming: *Sweet Thames, run softly, till I end my song.*

Im zimmer die Frauen come and go, sprechen von – ach, falsch Gedicht!

We went down the mountain and I heard my cousin shouting.

Yet once more, O ye Laurels, and once more! Now Voyager, much, much for thee is yet in store!

And I walk through the valley of the shadow of death and take a look at my life and realize there's nothing left.

Là, tout n'est qu'ordre et beauté: Nessun maggior dolore Che ricordarsi del tempo felice.

What's going on here? Where is this going? Madame
Sosostris, what gives?

Sweet, time for chess: England's number one pastime.

My king was killed, my queen violated, my rook and
brother left to wither. The rest is silence. (*dies*)

I see now the eyes of a familiar compound ghost, both
intimate and unidentifiable.

Già contento requïevi di grande ammirazione; ma ora
ammiro com' io trascenda questi corpi levi.

Time's winged chariot hurrying near! His hopes 'bove
wisdom, grace, and fear.

Glories, like glowworms, afar shine bright, but looked at
too near have neither heat nor light.

Why do you break me? It spoke! Is not a thing of beauty a
joy forever, what more do you need to know?

Jai Guru Deva Om, nothing's gonna change my world.

Lady Chatterley's Lover
by D. H. Lawrence

@EarlyBloomer69

Is it unusual that I had lots of sexual encounters starting from a fresh, ripe age?

I met a man today. Baby he's a rich man too! He's going off to war though.

My husband Clifford came back from war a cripple. Wheelchair. He can't get wood anymore :(

My man's deciding to be a little douche and start a writing career. He's pretty successful, but I'm pretty horny.

All his intello friends are coming over all the time. Borrrrrring. All they do is talk about books.

I'm having an affair with one of my husband's writer friends.

All he did during sex was talk to me about feelings and intellectual things. Does he think women like this? I just wanna fuck!

Our farmhand is so aloof and Romantic. I wanna get on that.

We're becoming friends. He's reluctant to talk to me because of 'class differences'. What a pussy.

We had sex in a shack. We shacked up, har har har. I've got plenty of sex puns left, don't worry!

We had sex again on the floor of a forest. We shared an orgasm. Cum together, right now, over me.

This is what I want. No brains, no talking, no sensitivity. Just str8 up fucking all day every day.

I'm def preggers with his baby.

My lover, Oliver, and I have such a purely physical bond. With bondage.

Oliver's bat-shit crazy wife came back and started talking smack about him.

He got fired from my family's property for the rumors his wife spread. I'm leaving my husband!

He won't give me a divorce. I would go Lorena Bobbitt on him if he had any use for his dick.

I'm so miserable. All I wish is that one day Oliver and I be together.

I wonder what Oliver is doing right now . . . probably plowing. I guess that's his job.

Jane Eyre
by Charlotte Brontë

@ToEyreIsHuman

I wish my parents had died impressively. Like Harry Potter; that kid's got one hell of an orphan story.

I have to live with my aunt. Total beo-tch. This is like Cinderella. Except no fairy godmother.

My aunt is sending me to a crap boarding school. It's like the ones you see in commercials for Save the Children on the History Channel.

The education is legit. Like we read books, but kids are dying of illness. This place is grimier than a hooker's snatch.

So apparently by not getting swine flu or TB I qualified for a teaching position?

Just got offered a job as a governess for a caddy single dad who needs to change womanizing ways. This would make a great Hugh Grant flick.

Romance, romance, this poppa Rochester wants to get in my pants!

We're in love. And to be married. This house is like a matchbox though, it keeps setting on fire. I wonder why?

This strange man has a secret about Rochester. He says that Rochester's got another wife locked in the attic!

There is legitimately a crazy black chick running around up here like she's playing a game of fucking animal charades.

LOL, her name is Bertha. I guess we know who was starting all those fires now though.

He says he was high in Jamaica and wanted to get tribal one night and got hitched. Haven't heard *that one* before.

I'm leaving. All this is much too crazy for me.

I ran away to a farm. This St John fellow wants to sleep with me, I think.

These farmhands are my cousins? And my dad left a huge inheritance for us. How convenient! Deus ex machina, win!

I'm going back to Rochester!

When I found him he was sitting in a pile of ashes crying. He's missing an arm and is blind.

The Kunta Kinte pyro bitch is dead. Maaaaawwwage!

Alice's Adventures in Wonderland
by Lewis Carroll

@AliceInTheSkyWithDiamonds

Like many book characters, I'm pretty bored. Oh! A white rabbit! Just like in *The Matrix*. That movie was pretty dope, if you're on drugs.

Down into the rabbit hole I go! Ohh, that's rich. I feel like Neo.

Is it OK to drink from a mysterious bottle that's been opened? What if there are Ruffies in it?

I don't know what's going on, but in a typically feminine manner I'll allow confusion and being flustered to make me cry up a storm.

Am I still the same little girl that I was before? I feel like my 'self' is being deconstructed. And in HD, to boot.

I asked a mouse how to get dry from all my tears. He gave me a dry history lesson. People are purposefully confusing my words.

I'm in the rabbit's house. Here's more mysterious juice. Should I drink it again? Oh what the hell. Hope I won't be sore afterward.

Why are people throwing rocks at me like I'm Mary Magdalene? I'm a little girl, not a biblical prostitute . . . er, Christ's wife.

I found a stoner Arab caterpillar. He made fun of me. Oh yeah? At least I'm not three inches tall with a case of the munchies.

At a tea party with a crackhead hat man. He's a schizoid. Insanity is part of his public image. After all, he put 'mad' in his name.

Sound has become distorted.

This land is terrorized by the Queen of Hearts. She's a card. Wouldn't it be funny if I just destroyed her army by shuffling them?

I'm in trouble. I'm not sure what I did. This is the worst day ever. I need a drink. Not from an unmarked bottle, though, no more of that.

Now I'm on trial. Another worst day ever. The queen stole my integrity and made me a felon. If I knew magic, I'd make her disappear.

If only I could grow large and crush them beneath me. Wait. I feel so strangely powerful, I'm huge. This courthouse is going down.

Oh, my sister is here. She's waking me for tea-time. Good, I'm home again.

A grinning cat, a tweeked-out hatter? A sadistic queen and a terrifying baby? This is the kinda shit that sends people to years of therapy.

God that was just insane. I need another adventure like that like I need a hole in the head.

The Tempest
by William Shakespeare

@Lolspero

Do you know what years on an island with a teenage daughter and a man-slave will do to you? No, not that.

Do you know hard it was dealing with that girl? She still thinks her period is a little man dying inside of her. Well, I guess it kind of is.

Isn't it conveniently ironic that all the people who ruined me have crashed on this very island? No! I did it with magic!

Oh my. This whole landing on the island plot is not going as planned. Instead it's a comedy of errors.

My slave is hanging out with a band of alcoholics. He's drunk. This is a mess of post-prom proportions.

Of course, my daughter says she's in love with some rockstar prince who promises love in return. She's a duchess, not a groupie!

It seems I still have semblance of control over this sprite, Ariel. Isn't that a girl's name, like the mermaid? He hates that joke.

Nothing's really going on, is it? This story is still pretty genius though. A story about nothing. Like *Seinfeld*.

Caliban is way drunker than before and is running around shouting about liberty. This is why you don't give slaves booze.

My daughter is very upset. She wants to marry. I fear she'll fall into drugs and adultery and come crawling back.

Actually, now that I see them together, I think that they are really in love. Unless this kid is a really good actor.

Kids and their devil music. Who knows anymore?

The BEST thing would be for more terrible things to happen, for the situation to deteriorate significantly. That's just what I need.

I can't deal with this nonsense anymore, I need an Advil and a Tums. Let's just put this to bed. THAT'S WHAT SHE SAID.

Today I told my daughter she could marry the rockstar kid.

I find it bizarre how now the world seems so frightening, and all the past matters not, and holds no bearing on anything.

These bricks, the sand, will all be gone one day. Time is so fugitive, and alas, so is life. Toss me in the shallows before I get too deep.

I shall cast this book of evil spells into the ocean.

Come on guys, give me a round of applause, wasn't I just amazing. Set me free, people. STAGE DIVE!!!! Catch me, please?

Madame Bovary
by Gustave Flaubert

@TheRealDesperateHousewife

I met a doctor today. He fixed my father's leg. He's coming back tomorrow, and the next day. He seems very dedicated to my father.

Suddenly, his wife says he can't come anymore. Why? It's not like he's attracted to my father.

Oh, wait. I totally know what's going on. It's like in those Harlequin novels I read.

The doctor's wife is dead. Soon he'll be at my doorstep. Yeah, we're married now. I'm a visionary. I should go to Vegas with this power.

He's a good husband, does everything right, but he's such a putz. He bumped into a bookshelf and caused a cascade of 200 books and an urn.

My sadness is bothersome. He says I need to change scenery. That will help like a trip to Italy cures TB. What I need is a good poking.

With child! I need a baby like I need a hole in the head. I definitely don't love this baby. Watch me go coat hanger on it.

What a drag it is getting old. Trying drugs. Also met a hot law student in town. He shares the same tastes as I do.

I wonder if men sometimes agree with your tastes just to get you into bed. Can't prove it, though. Never mind.

I can't do it! I must play the good housewife. My sense of morality is focused on duty rather than pleasure. Like in *Revolutionary Road*?

At least I'm a good person, at least I did what is right. At least I still have my virtue. I'm so miserable!

Today a man brought someone to my husband. He gave me the look. You know, the 'I want to get naked with you' look.

My husband agreed to let me go riding with the man. The hell with virtue.

You know what really turns me on? Sending filthy letters to my lover that my husband might see. It's risky, but really hot.

This is it: I'm going to leave my husband for my lover.

My lover doesn't want to run away, and complicate our lives. Was I just used for sex? I'm so terribly ill. Should I turn to God?

I've recovered all my strength. *God?* Turn to *God???* What was I thinking?

My life is awful. I'm going shopping. I want to buy a whole bunch on credit that I can't afford, and then declare bankruptcy.

Nobody will help me pay off my husband's debt. Not even the men I slept with. I'll eat poison and solve everybody's problems. Namely, mine.

Maybe I should have just left that poor doctor and his wife alone. Or been a good wife. W/e.

Death in Venice
by Thomas Mann

@GustavaelJackson

Like the elevator business, being a writer has its ups and downs. At least I made my last name sound aristocratic. That should get me laid.

I'm in Venice. There's a really old gent with make-up, fake teeth, and a wig hanging out with kids. Gross.

Thank God I get to stay in the nicest hotel in Venice. My wife just died. I keep having these weird encounters with men. I'm probably gay.

While walking in the hotel lobby, saw a little kid dressed in a sailor's uniform. Went from six to midnight. No Viagra needed.

Is it creepy that I'm following this kid in the hotel? He'd tell me if he felt weird, right? Should I buy him some candy to earn his trust?

I feel so separated from my desires. I think the best plan would be to dress like Michael Jackson and wander around Venice at night.

There's a health warning out about shellfish. Maybe the Jews were right.

Forget the Jews. I think the shellfish disease is like my boner for this kid. Yeah, that makes no sense.

173

The Italians say that the heat is the health risk. The Brits say it's cholera. I'm definitely listening to the inventors of penicillin.

I had a wet dream about the boy. It's time to start plan B: heavy, heavy stalking.

I worry that his parents have noticed me. They might issue an Amber alert if the child goes missing. Look out for gondola and child.

A barber convinced me to get this ridiculous haircut.

I must follow the child around town. I'm wearing some pretty, pretty rad clothes, if I may say so myself.

God I feel like shit. This fruit needs some fruit. Where the strawberries at?

Does this Polack kid even know who I am? I'm a big-time writer. He should be bowing to me. Literally.

I went to the beach and saw the boy I'm obsessed with fighting another kid. He got his ass kicked.

He's walking so tranquilly yet lustfully across the beach. He's so beautiful. He's so sensual. Look at that move: the moonwalk.

He's staring back at me. He's calling to me. Time to get my game on.

Suddenly I feel sort of weird. Maybe I ought to sit back down for a mome—

The Three Musketeers
by Alexandre Dumas

@d'ArtsDaMAN

It's time to go off into the world and follow my secondary dream and become a Musketeer. Apparently Jedis don't actually exist.

My father wrote me a rec letter to a captain. I lost it though, walking through a dodgy neighborhood. I bet those goddamn gypsies took it.

I met the captain today. He kinda treated me like a retard for losing the letter. I told him it was gypsies.

Uh, I may have gotten myself in a bit of a jam. Three Musketeers want to duel. Maybe I can take them?

Oh thank god Cardinal Richelieu banned duels. Almost died. The men want my help to kill the cardinal's men. Success=street-cred. Respekt.

I moved into my new digs today. Landlord is a grumpy old man. But his wife is fiiiinnne. I bet she married for the money.

I'm in love with this woman. The thought of her husband's saggy balls on her enrages me. Ah Constance, I dream of you at night.

Anne D'Autriche gave her diamonds to a duke. She could be in trouble if anyone finds out. Affairs are dangerous things.

I have to go on a diamond heist with my boyz. Athos is riding shotgun in the carriage.

The cardinal doesn't want us to have the stones. The musketeers decided to come though because they can't resist an adventure.

This cardinal is an evil, evil man. I bet he molests children. Time to start that rumor. Hope it sticks.

He kidnapped Constance! That fucker. My crew is gonna settle this.

Uh, so, uh, yeah. The rescue mission got complicated. Someone tried to kill me. Anybody know the best way to get rid of a body?

Apparently chopping off the head and dipping it in lye really works. Anybody read *Dorian Gray* or watched the *Sopranos*?

Anytime I go on an adventure with the Three Musketeers it turns out pretty hilariously. Bodies. They are serious little fuckers.

Porthos loves hookers though. Athos just wants to kick it on a farm.

Aramis wants to be a priest. Maybe I shouldn't have said all that nasty stuff about the clergy and little boys?

I'm gonna be an officer. Who knew this comedy of errors and bodies and sex could lead a poor boy to the title of officer?

Good things always seem to happen to the picaresque, don't they? Huh, sometimes life is just great. And I have these new friends.

Twilight
by Stephenie Meyer

@TheSecondSexist

I'm a teenage girl hoping to make friends at a new school in a new town. This should be *fascinating*! Oh, the weather sucks.

Wow, I'm all of a sudden really popular! This is a twist on the popular trope, isn't it? Oh, except this TOTALLY HOT guy says I smell bad.

He makes vulgar, offensive faces at me with his wanton, profound eyes. It's a cliché for me to fall. But why fight it? He is so very fine.

His face burns in my mind, and his hands seem crafted by God himself. I surrender.

I knew it. He just wants to be friends. (Notice how our relationship now seems unique for that reason.)

So I'm out walking and BAM, a car almost runs me over except that my new 'friend' shoves it out of the way with his bare hands.

Hey, anyone know what disease causes frigid skin, no need for food, and fear of light? Vitiligo universalis, like MJ had? Or is it death?

Pretty boy is a vampire. A bit obvious, but I still feel such a hormonal pull. He's pure pussy magnet.

Today I asked if he only liked me because of my tits. He said no, it's the smell of my blood. FML.

I like him 'cause he can read everybody's mind, but not mine. Maybe if he stopped staring at my tits . . . I don't care. He's so *dreamy*.

He says he's part of a no–killing–humans club. I hope he's not just saying this to get me into bed.

A bad vampire tried to kill me. He threatened to murder my mother, too. See? There IS some action in this story.

The bad vamp managed to bite me but my guy took him out and cured me. That was resolved quickly. Well, now we can be together.

I hope he doesn't bite during sex, that would really suck.

Oh, what do I tell my family? You can't introduce a vampire the same way you introduce an artist or a vagrant.

Since he is a vampire and I am a human, we'll have to work at our relationship. I am ready to make sacrifices, tho' not BE sacrificed. Clear?

My life lately has been a bit like a lonely girl's slightly creepy juvenile sex fantasy. But at least it really happened!!!

@YoungGirls: If a guy is hot enough, it's OK if he's also a blood–sucking creep. Completely subordinate yourself and accommodate him. Worth it.

Good thing this happened. Otherwise it would just have been a 40 yr old me, a bottle of cheap wine, and a whole bag of issues.

Moby-Dick
by Herman Melville

@greatwhitetale

Call me Ishmael. You could call me something else if you want, but since that's my name, it would make sense to call me Ishmael.

You know what I've always wanted to do? Work on a whale boat. I know I used to be a schoolteacher, but now I want to kill whales.

Met a man who says he can get me a job on the boat of a Captain Ahab. Traveling to Massachusetts to see.

My friend is a huge Polynesian harpoon-man. Seems all of Ahab's harpoon-handlers are such. Black spear-chuckers. Is that a problem?

On the boat. Something strange is going on. The Captain has a leg made out of a whale bone, and the crew seems terrified of him.

Captain obsessed with finding a whale called Moby Dick. Sounds like the meanest VD ever, if you ask me. Sorry. Old joke. Couldn't resist.

Ahab wants to hunt the whale. Starbuck says we must pursue profitable biz ventures. Argument ensued. Passion defeated capitalism. Go figure.

We set out. Follow @Starbuck, @Queequeg for long introspective soliloquies on the human soul. Or @Tashtego if you like adorable kittens.

The crew members really do reflect a gathering of all the spirits of the American experience. The 'Great' American experience?

Turns out Ahab had his own secret whale-boat crew here. One of the guys seems to be running the show, Rasputin-style.

Anyone follow @Pip? He's a smart guy. You think it's a joke that I tell you a little black man is brilliant? Nor smile so, twit.

Ran into other ships. Usually you get to play games, but Ahab is kind of a stuffed shirt and only asks, 'Oh hey. You seen Moby Dick?'

Queequeg is very sick. Please pray for him. This is serious. A coffin is being made for him at this very moment.

Never mind. The Q 'changed his mind' and will be living after all. The coffin is being retrofit into a lifeboat. Irony!

Ah ha! Someone has seen the white whale. It's about time everyone STFU about the human condition and we saw some ACTION.

Found the whale. We have begun to chase it. I suspect this clash of titans won't end well – for us.

And if his chest were a cannon, he would have launched his heart upon the whale. A bit self-defeating? Is that the point? Can you fathom it?

You'd think several boats of highly experienced whale-hunters wouldn't get schooled so badly by a big dumb whale. Oh well. Game over.

By game over, I mean everyone is dead but me. I'm adrift on what was supposed to be Queequeg's coffin. Like I said, IRONY.

It's kind of cold out here. Can somebody come pick me up? Please? Anybody . . .

Don Quixote
by Miguel de Cervantes

@DonQuixotic

People say that sleep deprivation, isolation, and too much reading have made me loopy. But I say nay! Nay!!!

I am a noble knight on a quest! Where is my trusty horse Rocinante – like Bucephalus with syphilis.

I am going full-creeper and giving a girl I love a special secret nickname without her even knowing about it.

I'll call her Dulcinea. Get it? Like Dulce del Coochayyyy.

A castle! No drawbridge. Pretty, pretty shabby if you ask moi. I'll ask the owner to knight me.

Is it bizarre that the owner of a castle is wearing patched overalls and has a corn husk pipe? Not very classy for a king.

He has knighted me! When the ladies ask who I am I'll say: *Quixote, Don Quixote.* Some traders have insulted my woman!

Fight didn't end well. Asshole neighbor brought me back home.

By Merlin's balls! A wizard, my niece claims, has taken our library away with magic. No more books for me :(

I promised some Sancho Villa mo–fo his own island if he helped me escape my niece so I could continue my quest.

I'm off on my journey!

WHAT THE FUCKING FUCKITY FUCK ARE THESE FUCKING GIANTS DOING. HOLY SHIT THEY HAVE 4 FUCKING SPINNING ARMS!!!

People say I have to pay my debts, but a Don don't pay squat!

Today a man said to me: *Don Quixote, I wanted to thank you for inviting me to your daughter's wedding on the day of your daughter's wedding.*

For Justice, we must go to Don Quixote. OK, enough Brando jokes.

So today Santo Paco, Pablo, Taco Bell – whatever his name is – brought three peasants and said they were Dulcinea and her maids.

Well Pablo Panzo, all I see are three whores!! LIAR!!!

Oh who am I kidding? This is a barber's bowl, not a helmet. And this horse blows.

I'm just some guy Alonso with illusions of grandeur. I don't feel so well. It's time to go to bed, time to sleep.

The Canterbury Tales
by Geoffrey Chaucer

@AprilFools

Road trip guys. Who's with us? Send me a parchment if you're in need of spiritual healing.

There's a Knight and his son. This guy's horse is like a tank. Better to tarry at its south end than court danger.

Next is the Yeoman, who's so tan and full of hair he lookes like Tom Hanks in *Cast Away*.

There's a Nun. She meprises Jews. It's awkward riding with an anti-Semite, because if we're bored she'll say, 'Let's kill some Jews.'

Also, she should be charitable, but she likes food. She's kind of a hypocrite. Didn't like my joke about the nunnery that blows up.

There's also the Friar. He HATES the Summoner, they're always talking shite before each other's necks.

Today the Friar was like, 'Hey, how about that Summoner, isn't he terrible?' Also he's a bit of a vagrant hobo. Basically he smells.

The Franklin just won't quit his talke – always interrupting people.

We also have a Haberdasheerere in our group. He's pretty boring, he makes socks. Not saying he's gay, though.

Oh and the Wyfe of Bathe. Talk about a woman who likes to be perced to the roote.

She got laide at her husband's funeral. A man filled her body upon the grave of her spouse. Ill in the head, no?

She probablie has many venereal sicknesses, her profession is being a wife. Everyone else has titles or jobs and she's just a wife?

The Miller likes sodomy. 'Tis all he talkes about. Ass-faugh this, colon-blast that.

The Miller likes not the quaint of a woman, but the arse. He tolde a joke about a red-hot poker.

And then there's Chaucer. He cannot tell a story to save his lyfe.

'Twas so bade that we had to shut him up. Can't he just give it a rest?

This trip sucks. I wish I had my N64. Mayhaps there'll be one in Canterbury. I hear there's also a meddlesome priest. Could be fun.

Sgt Pepper's Lonely Hearts Club Band
by The Beatles

@LetItTweet

It was 20 years ago today, Sgt Pepper taught the band to play. And by Pepper, I mean Brian, the Devil to whom we sold our souls for fame.

Anyone following @BillyShears? He replaced that friend we had, you know, our friend who is . . . no longer with us. But don't tell anyone.

It's a lot of fun just hanging out with your friends. Driving around, trying to be something, having a laugh, smoking a J, hallucinating.

This morning my kid went on and on about how I had to see the painting he did. Decided to take some LSD instead. I see Japanese women.

I was going to write a poem in dactylic tetrameter, but then I got high. Now I'm wearing glass around my neck, and I know why.

I used to be an abusive tyrant. Rockin' out, getting high, beating my woman. But now I'm better. Or at least no worse.

This morning my father told me I had to fix a hole in the roof. If I'm a carpenter, that makes him a walrus. Will the real Paul stand up?

But then Paul McCartney said – nothing, you idiot, Paul McCartney's dead. His corpse is locked in my basement.

My neighbor ran away from home this morning, before dawn. £20 says she ends up in the white slave trade.

My parents made me go to the circus. Saw an impressive horse, and a man who undertakes summersets through hoops of fire.

Meant to buy a car today. Got distracted and bought a sitar instead. It's a great instrument for faux depth, and looks like a large cock.

Asked my woman today if she would leave me if I became a 64-year-old raging alcoholic. Says don't worry: she won't live that long.

Saw a lovely woman, dressed like an army man. She's a meter maid. Calls herself Rita. I think I'll 'tow' her heart. Sorry.

Almost got laid whilst sitting on the couch with Rita's two sisters. Unless a foursome is in the works, this is pretty awkward.

Good morning, twittersphere!

So I'd like to keep on tweeting, but sadly I am told that it is time to go – the internet is only a sometimes thing, you know?

Stuck in traffic. Everyone rubbernecking this guy. Lordy, I believe I know him from somewhere.

Woke up, combed my hair, caught the bus, had correct change. Got to work on time, had a crap and a smoke and a nap. My life is average.

GGGGGGOOOOOONNNNNNGGGGG, bzz, bzzz, bzzzz – how long do you think we can hold this piano chord after the album's over . . . ?

Glossary

A guide to this book's obscure and esoteric terminologies and idioms for the benefit of luddites and old-timers that they may understand and enjoy the humor and wordplay herein contained.

<3

An icon of affection, representing a heart. Also used super-ironically because what kind of idiot uses the heart icon? Right?

</3

An icon of annoyance, representing a broken heart. Also used super-ironically because what kind of idiot uses the heart icon? Right?

'2' and other digits

To be understood as they are pronounced, rather than for their numeric value. Hence: 'I am going 2 the store', and 'This mysterious, poorly wrapped, ticking box is 4 you.' However, before this box can be opened, I must depart. 'See you l8r.'

AARP

Literally, American Association of Retired Persons, though often confused with American Association of Retarded Peoples, which bears a similar acronym. Its free, non-voluntary membership is a sure sign that you are now, in fact, old. No more denying it. Welcome to your Golden Years.

Amber alert

A California invention. When a child is abducted, the make, model, and license number of the abductor's car are displayed on large LED signs on the highway. This is presumably intended to make the perpetrator somewhat uncomfortable and perhaps compel him to pull over and contemplate the inevitable as he glances around awkwardly (and conspicuously) beneath the sign that describes him.

Ana/Mia/Bug

The three major body-image disorders, commonly referred to as 'anorexia nervosa', 'the ox hunger', and 'turning into a giant insect'.

BAMF

Literally, 'Bad Ass Motha' Fucka''. A certain type of gentleman whose sheer manliness, coupled with a disregard for law and society, inspires matrimonial amnesia in the women he encounters, and fear in all. As in, 'The guy is one BAMF – I can't tell if he's going to kill me, or just nail my wife!'

BDSM

Bondage-Domination Sadomasochism. All men, somewhere in the course of their sexual lives, have felt the impulse to get a bit aggressive. A small slap, a bit of a choke – in the heat of passion, these little impulses sometimes bubble to the surface and, sometimes, enhance the experience. However, some people, finding themselves possessed by an excess of this sentiment, venture further – chains, knives, beatings, burning – all met not only with their own pleasure, but with that of their partner as well. And thus, with these ideas in mind, and a bit of black leather, BDSM was born for all strange men's pleasure, and all the world's laughter.

BFF

Literally, 'best friends forever'. Actually, the use of this term is a reliable indicator that the user belongs to the 11- to 15-year-old girl/Jonas Brothers fan demographic, meaning your 'best friend' will be a 'total slut' when your boyfriend gets her pregnant in senior year. So much for forever.

Bone/bang/hit it/frogged etc.

The carnal expression of the spirit of Venus: to enjoy the consummation of affection, to make love, to get it on.

Brb

Be right back.

Bro

Just a typical guy. Enjoys shorts and a plain T-shirt. Likes a good game of pick-up basketball, or some Sunday afternoon football. Would love some barbeque and a beer. Will put Rohypnol in your drink and molest you in his frat house if he gets a chance.

Bromance

A bonding of the spirits of two heterosexual men. They go everywhere together, paint each other's nails, and stay up late drinking beers and sharing secrets. But there is nothing sexual about this relationship. Nothing. At. All.

BTW

'By the way', as in 'I throw this last bit in as an afterthought, hoping you won't notice it. But my guilty conscience forces me to at least *mention* that I have been copulating with your sister.'

Cock-block

To physically or metaphorically prevent another's phallus from arriving at its intended goal – usually by 'stepping on a brother's game' so that the lady of his affections never exposes the aforementioned goal to begin with.

Crunk

'Crazy drunk'. Similar to normal drunk, but possessing a daring young edge. To shout, 'I GET CRUNK EVERY DAY!' is to affirm one's place at the cutting edge of super-hip youth, whereas to shout, 'I GET DRUNK EVERY DAY!' is quite sad, and a reliable indicator of life-long alcoholism.

CTFO

'Chill the fuck out' – as in 'While my own expression may seem rather unsettled, I find your behavior unacceptably overwrought, and would suggest that, if you simply calm yourself, you may find this alleviates much of the situation's apparent intensity. CTFO, man.'

Douche

One of them new curse words them kids use nowadays. Implies the person in question is – worse than merely the exit point for feces – a device used for washing the pudenda.

DTF

'Down to fuck', as in 'Although I have only just seen that woman walk through the door, were she to approach and ask bluntly, "Would you like to return to my apartment and have sexual intercourse?", I would reply, "Indeed! I am, after all, down to fuck."'

Emo

'Emotional', specifically, the junior high school student fond of wearing box-framed glasses and all-black skinny jeans, and listening to Dashboard Confessional. Not old enough to be a hipster, or to have become fashionably apathetic à la Dostoevsky. The Emo Kid has arrived at the tender age of fourteen and has, as a consequence, realized that the upper-middle-class American private-school urban lifestyle is the most terrible and oppressive on Earth. They intend to let everybody know.

Epic fail

A popular internet term used to describe an ironic twist of events that, if the term is to be taken literally, is so immense it shall be sung about by poets for ages to come.

Flickr

A website in which several thousand aspirants to the crown of photography's 'next big thing' upload an unlimited number of images captured on the digital camera their parents bought them because going to that summer program really showed their commitment to photography. At least until next month.

FML

'Fuck my life'. Made popular by a website of the same name, this tag is used to denote little anecdotes of humorous misfortune. Most usually, the loss of a significant other, an affair, the blunders of one's parents, and the pitfalls of school and office politics.

Freud, Sigmund

Infamous cocaine addict and pederast. Also, a convenient stooge for any joke involving sex, one's mother, or (preferably) a combination of the two.

FTW

'For the win'. To commit to an undertaking (or to comment on another's) with great exuberance, expressing the grandeur of the task, and noting that you believe its successful execution will be an accomplishment of importance and note. 'I went to the tanning salon, and got TEN BOTTLES OF SPRAY-ON FTW.'

Ginger

An individual with orange or red hair. While there is nothing inherently strange about this, some find the idea that their pubic hair might also be bright red endlessly funny. As a result, an entire culture of comedy now exists surrounding these poor, ridiculous carrot-tops.

GTFO

'Get the fuck out', as in 'Sir! This building is on fire, and the men who have come to extinguish the flames are, in fact, assassins sworn on a blood oath to torture and kill you. Also, I need some privacy so that it is not awkward when your recent ex-girlfriend emerges from my bedroom wearing a sheet. In short, GTFO!'

Hipster

An indescribably happening youngster. Highly ironic, extremely elusive – whereas counter-cultures of times past proudly identified themselves as members of their particular subculture, a hipster is a scholar of half-understood memories from a community college philosophy elective, at once loudly advertising their hipster status in clothing, transportation, taste and cigarette choice, while loudly denying their status as a hipster, until one is led to believe that not one of them actually exists. Semiotics, man, yeah, that's deep.

iPhone

An electronic device that is, if you didn't already know (like, uh, what kind of loser are you?), basically the best thing bequeathed to mankind by kindly Steven Jobs from up on Mount Olympus. You didn't know that? Well, have you got a couple of hours? Because I've got some really cool apps I'd like to show you . . .

IRL

'In real life', as opposed to this imaginary one, which you have been enacting digitally as a way of compensating for your overwhelming physical, mental and artistic inadequacies.

Jerk It

To yank the chain, to do the Han Solo, to fasten the chin strap on the helmet of love, to take a load off, to be left to your own devices, to clean your rifle, to charm the snake, to flog the bishop, to 'do' your 'homework', to liquidate the inventory, to paint the pickle, to play five-on-one, to pull yourself by your own bootstrap, to scour the tower of power, to shake the sauce, to shake hands with Abe Lincoln, to stroke the carrot, to unload the gun, to yank the plank, to practice your wrist aerobics, to rub yourself until you have an orgasm.

Kick it

Much like 'hanging out' or 'chilling'. However, whereas those two terms refer to a state of relative contentment with present activities and company, 'kicking it' is an existential condition in which the homies are confronted with a lack of 'essence', and, as a result, are forced to confront the hollowness of their very lives. Inspires frustration and desire for more, but these feelings are rarely sufficient motivation to achieve transcendence. To be avoided at all costs.

LOL

Literally, 'laughing out loud!' The internet is a strange place, and in the format of cold text the important things – laughter, tears, tone and expression – are often lost. Luckily, quick acronyms such as this remedy the problem by allowing the other party to know that you are truly struck by their wit, and are involuntarily screeching in celebration of this fact.

Lulz

The essence of web-based comedy. When many individual acts of 'LOL', emanating from behind a million keyboards across the world, bind together in bonds of comedy and joy so mighty that only omnipotence could break them, a network is formed that brings mirth to all who seek it. This is the Lulz.

Mack

To practice the art of seduction. To speak with grace and charm, usually to a member of the fair sex, such that she might relinquish her girlish fears and take one as a lover. To keep it real with the bitches, as it were.

MILF

A woman of a certain age with whom one would enjoy a good roll in the hay. Literally, 'Mother I'd like to fuck', although such language really isn't the sort of thing you should use around your or anybody else's mother. Then again, neither is your penis.

Nads

A man's testicles. There is nothing funny about these.

NM (or N/M)

'Never mind': 'As I have already wasted enough of my and your time with words now rendered irrelevant, I cannot bring myself to waste yet more with a multi-syllabic notification of the retraction. Hence, NM.'

OMG

'Ah, dear Providence! In your gentle stewardship of the Earth, I am unnerved that such a situation as the one I now confront could be your handiwork, and thus, I cry out reflexively to you for explanation and comfort: Oh my god!'

Peace, bitches

'Farewell, my gentle companions.'

Pinko

A Communist. Or perhaps a socialist. I'm not sure what the difference is, but they're both no-good, anti-American, if you ask me.

Pls

Please. Without the vowels, it loses a bit of the sincerity and effort one would normally associate with a request that requires polite language, but perhaps the other party appreciates such brevity as it allows them to embark upon the desired act more quickly.

Preggers/pregz

The lady is with child.

Punk'd

To walk into what one believes is an actual catastrophe, but which ends with a dog-faced bro jumping out from behind a bush, laughing and waving a camera as you realize your folly on national television.

PWNT/PWND

Technically a contraction of 'owned', with the 'o' intentionally mistyped as a 'p'; as in 'bested' or 'I have defeated you.' Colloquially, 'I am a child/video game enthusiast/fraternity brother and could think of nothing more clever to say. But yet, as it is, I am still your superior in the battle of wits at hand.'

ROFL

Sometimes a simple 'LOL' is not enough. Upping the comedic ante to a much higher level, 'rolling on the floor laughing' at first challenges the honesty that is vital to textual expressions of emotion. How, after all, can one type if one is indeed on the floor, prostrating oneself before the Gods of Comedy? One realizes quickly, however, that such expressions are metaphorical; the typist still sits safely behind his keyboard, while it is his soul that turns and turns upon the ground, possessed by the spirit of mirth.

Shawty, in the act of 'gettin' lo'

Shawty, a sexually liberated woman of striking and enticing appearance, making herself low, presumably in proximity with the dance floor, so as to demonstrate her virtuosic mastery of the physical motion that could be applied back at your place.

STFU

'Shut the fuck up'. Really, do.

Tweet

To emit a small chirping sound, in the manner of a bird. Used to describe the posting of a message on Twitter.com – 'Of course I know about Todd Palin's daughter – I tweeted about the whole scandal yesterday! Aren't you following me?'

TXT

To text, as in to send a text message. This act is most often performed on the road, because to speak on a cell phone while driving is generally illegal, while looking down at a small screen and typing is, obviously, much safer.

Web MD

Technically, a website replete with medical knowledge from both textbooks and professionals that greatly aids in the dissemination of useful medical information, and that serves as a useful alternative to the long waits and steep bills occasioned by visiting an actual doctor. More commonly, a place where hypochondriacs may exacerbate their condition and spend hours obsessing over the possible ways they might be dying that day.

W/e

Whatever.

'Word up!', 'Represent!', etc.

A series of semi-intelligible phrases most often yelled by Anglo-Saxons aspiring for minority status. Translates roughly to 'I am here! Yes, look at me!'

WTF

'What the fuck?!', as in 'I am quite shocked to discover you, my wife, in the bed of my fiercest friend and dearest rival! Indeed, my reaction is a combination of surprise, confusion, rage and sorrow. What the fuck?!'

YouTube

Similar to television, except free, two-directional, accessible to everyone, and has more than a million shows to watch. However, there is still nothing good on right now.

A few lines

Cocaine.

Bump

Cocaine.

Bushbait

Cocaine.

Colombian marching powder

Cocaine.

Miracle powder

Cocaine.

Nose candy

Cocaine.

Snorts

Cocaine.

Snuff

Cocaine.

Twitter format

@Username

A person's pseudonym on Twitter.com. When used within a post by someone else, this directs the message at them.

D Username

Similar to @Username, except a direct message – more private.

#words

A hash tag (#) marks a post as being in a certain group or relating to a certain theme. Posts that share the same hash tag can be found listed together.

Acknowledgments

Much could be said about how a book of any sort is not a solo effort. Pages and pages could be burned with ink, celebrating the contributions of those who gave aid and comfort to us as we embarked on this journey to bring the knowledge of the ages, and perhaps a little smile, to those kind enough to venture through this text. However, if we have learned anything from this process, it is that our day and age is defined by a wit borne of brevity, and for that reason, we feel compelled by Zeitgeist to keep this simple.

This book would not be possible without: Brian DeFiore, John Siciliano, Yen Cheong, Will Hammond, Joe Pickering, Mary Pachnos, André and Susan Aciman, Susan Peterson, and David Rensin.

We would also like to thank the following people: Michael and Phillip Aciman, Michael Berlin, Elise Biggers, Hana Hawker, Rebecca Roberts, Emily Beyda, Matthew and Nicholas Engel, Harry May-Kline, Marcella Zimmerman, Djobi Rojas, Ulysses Pascal, Arpy Sarkissian, Amy Chou, Daniel Gaines, and the Lord Jesus Christ, Amen.

And of course a special thanks to all the great writers – both those included and those excluded from our work – from Homer, to Joyce, to Rowling, whose pens and quills have helped guide our minds on the daring, righteous path of enlightenment.

Index